Words of praise
and the Shirley

"Bursting with humor but steeped in reality, Toni's books offer a delightfully balanced way to see this crazy world we all habitate."
                                                    —Stephen R. Covey

"The SHIRLEY YOU CAN DO IT! books offer a realistic, warm-hearted approach to everyday living, with a twist of humor that is uniquely Toni Brown. I love a book that has me laughing and crying . . . all on the same page. Toni's books will move you to that, page after page."   —Marie Osmond

"It is a small treasure with a large impact. It can be read in one evening and savored for many nights to come . . . VALIDATE ME QUICK is like finding a new friend that understands how the daily frustrations of life can sometimes become overwhelming."   —*Davis County Clipper* (Utah)

"Witty and captivating . . . Recommended to all those weary moms and wives who feel they are lacking appreciation."
                              —*Horizon News* (Salt Lake City, Utah)

"Until now, there has never been a series of books written especially for women by a woman. The idea is a singular one in a saturated market . . . As the readers get to know Shirley, they will discover that they know a little bit more about themselves. Her powerful, humorous messages have a universal appeal to all women."   —*Park City's E.A.R.* (Utah)

"The well-placed humor and reaffirming quality of the work make it appealing . . . an entertaining book about self-discovery and the female experience . . . the perfect gift for any woman."   —*Salt Lake Observer*

Validate Me Quick; I'm Double-Parked!

Toni Sorenson Brown

St. Martin's Paperbacks

VALIDATE ME QUICK; I'M DOUBLE-PARKED!

Library of Congress Catalog Card Number: 95-71765

ISBN: 0-312-97005-6

Printed in the United States of America

Token Ink edition / November 1995
St. Martin's Paperbacks edition / January 2000

10 9 8 7 6 5 4 3 2 1

For every woman whose arms are often too tired to reach around and pat herself on the back, for attempting the extraordinary amid the ordinary.

Let him go where he will, he can only find so much beauty or worth as he carries.

Emerson
"Culture"
The Conduct of Life (1860)

Validate Me Quick; I'm Double-Parked!

The shrill screech of the alarm shattered the dark morning silence. Shirley shot up in bed. "Who died?" she screamed into the buzzing telephone receiver.

Her husband, Stan, grunted and jabbed her in the ribs with his elbow. "It's the alarm clock."

Reality slowly came into focus.

Five A.M.

Monday morning.

The start of a new woman.

Already Shirley could feel last night's resolve waning. Five A.M. was an hour for the insane and the "in bed." Shirley placed herself comfortably under both categories. Still, she had promised herself, so Shirley rocked the phone receiver back onto the hook and slapped the snooze button on the alarm. Then she groaned and stretched, inadvertently digging Stan with her jagged big toenail.

He moaned and turned away.

I meant to get that clipped, she thought groggily.

He rolled to the edge of the bed, taking the

warmth of the quilt with him. "Shirley, you're not getting up now?" Stan muttered it more to himself than to her.

Shirley sighed. "Uh, huh."

"The start of *another* new you, huh?"

"That's right, sweetheart. The start of *another* new me."

"Ouch!" he yelped suddenly. "You really do need to trim your toenails."

It was still pitch-black outside when she finally managed to drag herself from the bedroom to the adjoining master bathroom. Shirley flipped on the light switch. BIG mistake. It felt like someone had just yanked her eyeballs from their sockets, pulled them far enough to challenge their elasticity, and then let 'em flip back into place.

"So this is what early-morning euphoria is like," she mumbled, splashing cold water on her sleep-swollen face.

"What did you say?" asked Stan.

"Nothing. Go back to sleep."

"Then turn off the light so I can."

"Sorry, Stan." Shirley pushed the bathroom door closed to leave her husband in the warmth and comfort of the pre-dawn shadows.

By 6:00 A.M. the sun was still not up, but Shirley was wide-awake. She had already made it through the first three goals on her "Things to Do Today" list, more than that if you counted getting dressed and brushing her teeth. Shirley was actually feeling pretty good about herself this morning, a rather foreign feeling for this woman.

No, today wasn't her first attempt at becoming a new woman, far from it. But today was the first day of *this* effort, and this time would be different, she assured herself. This time she would tackle her goals with self-confidence and courage. This time she would turn a corner and not meet a dead end. She tried to summon up that seventh sense every woman has to reassure her of her direction, but most of Shirley's senses were still asleep.

So Shirley stretched her hands out in front of her and made a triangle between her thumbs and fingers. It was a trick she had seen Grasshopper on *Kung Fu* do many times to help him focus. "Today my mind, my body, and my spirit will be in harmony," she chanted aloud, sounding neither Asian nor wise. "Surely, you can do this," she whispered aloud. Then she chuckled. "*Shirley*, you can do this!"

When 7:00 A.M. rolled around, the rest of the family was just stumbling from slumber. She couldn't help feeling a twinge of nervous anticipation. What would they think when her husband and children saw all that she had accomplished? There was her exercised and showered body (a major work still in progress), the makeup (lips actually lined and dark circles mostly concealed), the neatly trimmed and polished toenails and fingernails, the vacuumed carpet (with no ground-in Cheerios or even footprints crushed into the shag), and then there was the crowning masterpiece—the sparkling kitchen, the table set with real linen napkins and spot-free Sunday dishes, fresh-squeezed orange juice in frosted mugs, and healthy home-baked oat bran muffins and steaming cracked wheat cereal sweetened with honey. It was an early morning feast worthy of royalty.

Shirley stood at the bottom of the staircase anxiously awaiting the delight that was sure to register on the regal faces of her family as they raced down the stairs.

"Where's my math homework?" shouted Sean, whizzing past Shirley in a whirl.

"It's on the desk, dear, and good morning to you, too," she answered, telling herself, The boy is only seven—his behavior can be excused.

Next came Samantha. "The table looks nice. What's for breakfast?"

"Orange juice, muffins and hot cereal," Shirley announced proudly.

"Healthy stuff, huh? Sounds delicious." Samantha managed that whiny sarcasm that only a twelve-year-old can.

"Got any toast—*white* bread?"

Breakfast was even more than Shirley could have dreamed. Her family acted like royalty all right, and she felt just like a peasant woman. Custom-fit for a life of servitude.

Her husband, Stan, enjoyed his bacon, eggs and white toast. "I'm just not in the mood for cracked wheat." He had attempted an apology. Then he kissed her on the cheek. It was one of those puckered, dry, duty kisses. "Shirley, you've outdone yourself this morning."

"My feelings exactly," she agreed.

Samantha enjoyed her white toast layered in butter and honey. She did agree to sample the orange juice. "This tastes different," she whined without effort, "and it's got feathers floating in it."

"It's pulp, not feathers," Shirley corrected her, calmly digging her freshly painted nails into her own palms. Breathe deep, she told herself. After all, it was only breakfast they were attacking. If that was true, then why did Shirley feel like she was the target?

"The juice tastes different because I spent almost an hour squeezing a dozen oranges so that you would have fresh orange juice this morning," she explained between gritted teeth.

"You don't have to whine, Mom," said Samantha, gulping the juice anyway. "I just like the frozen kind better—you know, the stuff that comes in a can. It tastes better."

"I'll remember that next time."

Sean, bless his seven-year-old heart, ate three of his mother's oat bran muffins smothered in butter and fresh strawberry jam. He wasn't in the mood for cracked wheat cereal or orange juice with feathers floating in it, either. But he did think the frosted goblets were a "cool" effect—especially when Shirley failed to lunge quite fast enough to keep Sean from pouring steaming hot microwaved cocoa into his.

"I'll help you clean it up," Stan said of the shattered glass mess.

"It's okay. I can do it. Just get ready for work, or you are going to be late."

"I've got plenty of time," he said, separating himself from his wife with a wall of the morning newspaper. "Besides," he said from somewhere behind the sports section, "I thought you wanted to enjoy a leisurely breakfast together as a family this morning."

Shirley reached across the table for a piece of broken glass. A lethal weapon in the wrong hands.

"I'll help you clean up Sean's mess," volunteered Sara, who was three years old, and at the moment, aeons more mature than Shirley.

"No, honey, you could cut yourself," her mother cautioned just as blood spurted from Shirley's index finger.

By the time 10:00 A.M. rolled around, Stan was off to work. Samantha and Sean were at school. Sara was coloring creatures she had made out of the cracked wheat box. Turned out that nobody was in the mood for such a healthy, hearty cereal. Not even Shirley. But she did manage to finish off the muffins and the rest of the strawberry jam. She also downed the rest of the freshly squeezed orange juice and had to silently acknowledge the resemblance between the tiny pieces of pulp and feathers. From now on, the only competition that frozen concentrate would face for the family's morning beverage would be a diet Coke—Shirley's personal choice for that pick-me-up and get-me-started drink.

She did the obligatory once-over on the house—setting the dishwasher in motion, making sure all the toilets were flushed and the stairs were free of dangerous toys that could trip a person. Domestic duties done, Shirley then opened her laptop computer and began poking at the keyboard with her Snoopy-bandaged index finger. Suddenly she felt herself age by a decade as her body slumped and sagged.

Why does my life have to be experienced in such extremes? she wondered. This morning's high and this minute's low. It seemed like she was always tipping one end of the scale or the other. Why couldn't she just manage to enjoy the measures in between? The question was a good one and she considered it for some time. Her doctor had ruled out her self-diagnosis of a bipolar disorder. "Some people are simply more prone to mood swings," she had told Shirley. "What you need to do is learn to relax and savor life minute by minute."

For that bit of medical advice, Shirley had paid a fifty-dollar deductible and been forced to fill out a half dozen medical forms. So . . . if she didn't need Prozac or psychiatric care, what did she need? Some way to recognize and appreciate those precious measures along life's scale.

Shirley sat staring at the blank computer screen, feeling a little profound, but still mostly down. That is when she heard the voice. It was a man's voice, rich and resonant. She shook her head to clear her thoughts, then listened to be certain she wasn't going completely mad. Nope. The voice was real. Sara had turned the television on and the sound was booming from down the hallway.

"For any woman who longs to feel worthwhile, appreciated, and complete—stay tuned."

Shirley was in front of the TV in a heartbeat.

"Sounds like this is one program I can't miss," she said to Sara, adjusting the volume on the television and falling back into the comfort of the couch cushions.

"But, Mommy, I wanted to watch cartoons," protested Sara; she gripped the remote control in her tiny fist. "*Scooby-Doo* is coming on in a minute and he is going to rescue his friends from Zombie Island."

Shirley quickly, but gently, pried the remote control from her daughter's clutch. Shirley felt that she was the one in need of rescuing. "Sweetheart, you can watch *Scooby-Doo* any time. Right now, there is a program on television that Mommy really *needs* to watch. You can sit right next to me and color in your Scooby-Doo coloring book."

"But it's old."

"Next time I go to the store, I'll buy you a new one. Deal?"

"New crayons, too?"

Shirley nodded.

"Deal, then." Sara shook her mother's hand and grinned.

For the next sixty minutes, Shirley sat mesmerized while Sara continued to color. She was so engrossed in the program that Shirley didn't even notice when Sara traded her crayons for the lip-liner pencil that had been so enormously *in*effective that morning.

The infomercial man was captivating. This male Ph.D. had obviously taken his studies on women's emotions very seriously. Without ever having met her, he was able to pinpoint Shirley's problem—right there from the television screen he spoke to her insecurities and feelings of worthlessness. What Shirley was lacking in her life was VALIDATION.

How could a stranger know her so well? He was dead center. Right on. It was true that no one made Shirley feel worthwhile, appreciated, or complete. She lacked that stamp of approval that somehow made her a legitimate success.

The man combined his Ph.D. skills with powerful preaching as he had Shirley interacting with the thirteen-inch TV screen.

Could she feel the truth in his words?

"Yes!"

Did she ache to feel loved and appreciated by those she loved and appreciated?

"Oh, yeah."

Was she a broken woman?

"I'm not so sure."

Okay, if not broken, was her spirit at least bruised?

"Absolutely."

Was her goal to feel whole and happy instead of fragmented and depressed?

"You bet."

Did she want the pain to go away?

"Yes!"

Did she want it to leave right away?

"This minute."

Was she willing to pay a price to have that pain removed and replaced by joy?

"What kind of price?"

A price that was minuscule in comparison for the change it would wreak in her life.

"How minuscule?"

So minuscule, it could be divided into three easy payments that would automatically be charged to her credit card.

"Okay."

Shirley felt a tiny tug at her sleeve. "Are you okay, Mommy?"

Shirley tipped her chin. "I think so, honey."

"You're talking to the TV, Mommy. That man can't really hear you. He's not really in the box."

"Oh," sighed Shirley.

When the 1-900-VAL-DATE number flashed

across the screen, Shirley had regained enough composure to recognize it for what it was. But she was desperate, and $3.95 per minute sounded like a reasonable investment at the moment.

She felt a little foolish dialing the number, and almost hung up when she heard a recorded message announce, "Stay on the line for information that is guaranteed to change your life for the better."

Shirley wanted her life to change for the better, so she stayed on the line. She felt like she had been hanging for so long now anyway, what was another minute or two?

Seven dollars and ninety cents later, she spoke to an actual person. Twenty-two minutes, or a week's worth of groceries later, Shirley had the basic formula for validation. It was simple really. Almost silly, it was so juvenile. But if it would make her feel better about herself, what did she have to lose?

The formula for validation seemed elementary enough. In a few weeks, she would be receiving a specially designed parking validation coupon in the mail. If she didn't want to wait for it to arrive, she could acquire a real parking validation or make a coupon of her own. Then she was supposed to divide it into pieces like a jigsaw puzzle. On each piece, she was supposed to write down the name of a person from whom she sought validation. When she finally felt validated by a person, she was to put the puzzle together piece by

piece until it was complete. Abracadabra—
Shirley, too, would be complete and validated.

"I can do this," she assured herself aloud. "Can
Mommy borrow a page from your coloring book?"
Shirley asked Sara.

"Will you stay in the lines this time?"

"Oh, I don't want to color it."

"What do you want it for, then?"

"I'm going to make a puzzle," she answered her
daughter's query. Then she noticed that Sara had her
lips, teeth, and most of her fingernails covered with
Shirley's Magical Mauve lip liner. Normally,
Shirley would have lost her temper at this point, but
all she could do at the moment was smile and wonder what else had been going on right under her
nose that Shirley was oblivious to.

Sara asked, "What kind of a puzzle?"

"I'm going to make a special puzzle so that I can
feel validated."

Sara's little brow furrowed. "Will it hurt?"

Shirley smiled, licked her thumb, and began to
smudge the lip liner from her daughter's face. "I
sure hope not, honey. I sure hope not."

Shirley was sure her list would be a short one.
First there was Stan. She loved him desperately, but
he never even came close to understanding, let alone
appreciating all that Shirley did in any given day. A
big part of Shirley's initial attraction to Stan had
been his keen ability to feign stupidity. No. That

was not accurate—or fair. Stupid was not the right word. Maybe naive. No. Innocent? Hardly. Clueless was more like it. Back when Shirley had first met Stan, he had come across as a big kid that required at least a second explanation to most things.

Those were their college days when Shirley relished any excuse for explaining and practicing all that she was learning as a psychology major. Stan may have come across as the typical "big dumb jock," but she soon realized he was just putting on an act for her benefit. She had been so naive and gullible that it took her too long to realize that Stan was not really a jock. And not really dumb. All of his "Huh?" questions were, as he later confessed, just an excuse to get her attention.

Shirley smiled a sad smile when she tried to recall the last time Stan had sought her attention. There was plenty of love and devotion in their marriage, but there was also a lot of taking each other for granted as well. She knew it worked both ways, but right now Shirley was focused on getting herself validated, and Stan's name topped her list.

During their courtship, Shirley had actually admired Stan's ability to tune out his surroundings and focus on one thing at a time. It had worked as part of his clueless character. But now when Stan was focused on a football game or a book, Shirley felt that she was the one being ignored or excluded. Could she ever recapture his peak attention span?

Shirley had once read about a woman who wanted to get husband's attention, so she cleaned the house, cooked his favorite meal, and then met him at the door lathered *only* in whipped cream and a cherry. She captured his attention all right. Only she forgot one little detail; she neglected to turn off the television. Seems the New York Knicks were battling Michael Jordan. The woman claimed she could not recall who won the basketball game that night. All she could remember was that she lost.

Shirley did not ever want her union with Stan to end up in one of those magazines under "Is There Any Hope For This Marriage?" Then she thought about it. Seemed like she had heard those magazines paid top dollar to hear about desperate women and their desperate measures.

She shook her head to clear the confusion. Stay focused, she told herself. Validation.

Shirley wasn't about to meet Stan at the door lathered in whipped cream, but she would find a way to help him realize how valuable she was to the quality of his life. She didn't expect him to give up sports or reading or any of his other interests. She just wanted to be one of his interests. Okay, his primary interest. After all, he was hers—wasn't he?

Stan did not begin to comprehend the fact that she had put her career on hold to help raise their family. She ran the house. Nurtured the kids. Supplemented their income. Cooked. Cleaned. Chauf-

feured. And as far as the whipped cream thing—
well, their sex life had benefited from a can or two
of the kind that could squirt clear across the room,
and who was the one who had scrubbed it off the
walls afterward? Certainly not Stan.

No. Stan did not validate her.

But he would.

Next came the kids. If only they could grasp the
fact that all her loony behavior like screaming and
scolding was not because she was insane, but
because she loved them. She knew that they would
have to wait until they had children of their own to
fully appreciate the crazy love that drives a parent;
until then Shirley would be ecstatic if she could
only *feel* their budding appreciation. Their validation.

Putting it into words made it seem crazy, but
Shirley told herself she did deserve their respect.
Their appreciation. She was their mother. It was
entitled to her by default. She laughed out loud.
Who was she kidding? These kids ranged in age
from just beyond toddler to just before puberty. She
might as well run for President. Then at least the
people would recognize her value as a servant of the
people. Right now she served her children, all right.
Every minute of every day. They needed to recognize and honor the role she played in their lives. Not
servant. Not slave. Mother.

How do you seek validation from a three-year-old? Probably the same way she would have to seek it from Stan.

Good thing Shirley still had that 1-900 number.

It was three days later before Shirley had completed her validation puzzle list. The length of the list surprised her, but a few of the names that turned up on it actually stunned her. Some had been written, then erased, rewritten, scratched out, and then inked in again.

Besides Stan and the kids, there was Shirley's mother, Lena. The woman might as well wear a black robe and carry a gavel. Every day of Shirley's life she had brought down judgment. Usually not in Shirley's favor. Shirley knew the woman had not had an easy life, but did that give her the right to be so critical—so judgmental?

Shirley loved her mother and probably understood her better now than she ever had, but theirs was a relationship that would have perplexed Freud. Love. Hate. Hate. Love.

No—hate was too strong a word, and maybe love wasn't strong enough.

All mother-daughter relationships were complicated, Shirley assured herself. Daughters needed to be validated by their mothers, no matter how old they were. Shirley had never felt her mother's validating strength. As much as she hated to admit it, Shirley needed her mother to still recognize her achievements and to praise them once in a while. Every kid needs to see her art work hung proudly on the refrigerator door by a proud parent, thought Shirley. That's all I want. That's all I need. Admitting it to herself made Shirley feel somehow closer to her mother, even though they had not spoken in weeks.

Maybe getting her mother's validation wouldn't be such a struggle. In any event, Shirley felt warranted in giving her mother a significant piece of the puzzle.

Shirley's old boss was one of those names she wrote with a hesitant hand. She mused aloud to little Sara as they sat at the kitchen table, carefully crafting the validation puzzle. Each piece was meticulously written and designed. That's because Shirley left most of the artwork up to Sara.

"Why don't you draw the puzzle shapes, Mommy?"

"Because Mommy can't even draw a stick figure."

"What's a stick figure?"

"It's a person."

"But people aren't made out of sticks."

"I know, honey. But this puzzle is just a bunch of shapes. The shapes don't really mean anything."

Sara picked up the piece that was labeled with Shirley's old boss's name. "Look, Mommy—this piece looks like a frowny face!"

"You're right, Sara; it does." Shirley could not help thinking how apropos the piece was. She took it from Sara and noticed that her hands were trembling. Even after all the time that had passed since he had fired her, the man could still make Shirley shake and feel sick to her stomach.

"Maybe I need more than a do-it-yourself course," she confessed to Sara.

Sara looked at her mother and handed her a yellow crayon. There were also bright markers and a rainbow of colored pencils from which she could choose to provide individuality to each piece of the validation puzzle. All of the names were written in bold black Magic Marker, but some were definitely larger and bolder than others.

Shirley set the yellow crayon down and reached for a different color. Then she began to outline the name of her former boss.

"How come that piece of your puzzle is darker than the others?" Sara wanted to know.

Dark was a good word to describe that piece and all that it represented.

Shirley continued to outline the name over and over again until only she could read it.

Long after Sara's interest in the puzzle had waned and she was watching *Scooby-Doo*, Shirley remained at the table. Another name she wrote with trepidation was also from her past. It was Shirley's tenth-grade English teacher. The woman had been Shirley's mentor, although Shirley was painfully aware that the teacher never considered her a prized pupil.

She still had the report on Chaucer, the one with the teacher's blood-red cursive handwriting across the top stating, "There is no shame in being average. Grade C."

That one message had left an indelible impression on Shirley's young mind—on her life. It was now way past time to get that grade raised. To set the record straight.

There were other names that seemed to naturally belong to the puzzle. Names of friends and family. Wanting to feel validated by those people made sense. But why, wondered Shirley, were there pieces of her most personal puzzle devoted to her hairstylist, the family milkman, and the house cleaner?

Why did she care what near-strangers thought of her?

Why did it matter? It wasn't like she was coiffured by her hairstylist daily, weekly, or even monthly. She was lucky to get a clip and curl three or four times a year! As for the milkman, he came three times a week, but so what? Shirley had only spoken a few dozen words to him in her entire life.

Why did she need validation from these people who barely brushed her life? Why did what they thought of her matter?

It made no sense.

Shirley had no answers. She only knew it mattered very much to her, and so even though the pieces were small, they were still important to the completion of her validation puzzle.

When Shirley had completed drawing the puzzle, she carefully cut out each piece with Sara's blunt scissors. She could not help noting that some of the pieces did seem to take on shapes of their own. Her old boss's looked like a frown, her mother's resembled an ashtray, and Stan's reminded her of a heart.

Every step of the project so far had been cathartic. But there had been no real contact with any of the names in the puzzle. No confrontations.

Shirley hated confrontation.

Maybe this is all I need, she thought, feeling a little like she was on the third day of antibiotics—getting better, but not well.

Okay, I'll do it. I'll go to each one of these people and seek validation.

But what if they won't . . .

She quickly caught her negativism and squelched it. Then she placed each puzzle piece in an envelope and tucked it in her lingerie drawer—under the skimpy red and black teddies that she still kept, though she hadn't worn them in a decade.

Two weeks later, that envelope remained untouched, still at the bottom of the drawer.

There had been no more 5:00 A.M. wake-up calls, but the metamorphosis of Shirley was definitely under way. While the outside remained the same, she could feel a transformation taking place within. Those deep rumblings of her spirit were frightening and at the same time, exhilarating. What would the "validated" Shirley be like, she wondered?

There were moments when she failed to suppress, but actually addressed, her hopes and fears with unharnessed imagination. That's when she saw herself happy, laughing carefree with her head back. That's when she saw herself thin. As long as she was shedding the shackles of unworthiness, she might as well shed some of the extra weight she carried underneath her clothes. She had seen overweight people on talk shows and they seemed happy with their big bodies and their broad lives. Still, whenever Shirley allowed her imagination to soar, the picture she painted of herself was always a little thinner than the one she saw when she looked in the mirror.

The "fantasy Shirley" was also surrounded by a happy family in a clean house.

Reality always reared its dubious head and brought Shirley right back to the sticky kitchen table that was capable of claiming your elbows if you set them down for too long. Somewhere between fantasy and reality, there had to be a world where Shirley could find validation.

If Stan and the kids suspected the change that was under way, they gave no indication. They seemed happy in their oblivion.

Cold cereal and white toast—actually, anything that could pop from the toaster—sufficed for breakfast. No one seemed to miss the "feathers" in the orange juice or the steaming cracked wheat cereal.

The minimum weekly exercise requirements

Shirley had set for herself were sometimes met and sometimes let go.

She kept a little journal, but found that if she attempted to chart her progress on a daily basis, it was too disheartening. However, if she allowed herself some time and space, Shirley could see that she was headed in the right direction.

Maybe she just needed to stay pointed forward and keep moving. Perhaps this validation thing was as silly as it seemed at times.

Maybe this whole thing was not necessary, she about had herself convinced.

Then the doorbell rang.

"Mom! I was just thinking about you—sort of."

Lena half-hugged her daughter. "That's nice, I suppose." Then she quickly pushed past Shirley. Lena was wearing wearing a black skirt and a bright-yellow jacket. High heels. Shirley still had on her pajama bottoms, but at least they were mostly covered by one of Stan's old flannel shirts.

"I was in town for a doctor's appointment. I thought I'd stop by and see the children. Where are they?"

Lena looked around the kitchen and focused on the table. It was still covered with breakfast dishes, although it was practically lunch-time. Good thing Shirley had eaten the last blueberry Pop-Tart and had tossed the package into the garbage. Now the only evidence of Shirley's malnourished family was a spilled box of Cap'n Crunch.

Shirley tried to ignore the sneer that she was sure

she saw register on Lena's face. Shirley almost always kept the house clean and orderly, but not on the days her mother popped in. Did the woman have spies?

"Mom, it's Wednesday. You know the kids are at school. Now, what did you say about a doctor's appointment? What's the matter? Are you sick?"

"Don't worry, dear," Shirley's mother answered, gingerly picking up a half-eaten Pop-Tart Shirley had missed. Lena dropped it onto a dirty plate and then stepped back, as if it were a grenade about to explode. "So where's little Sara?"

Shirley could not help it. She followed her mother's lead like a well-trained pet. She started cleaning the kitchen table, piling all of the partially eaten breakfast treats onto a plate and then into the garbage. She scooped the spilled Cap'n Crunch into a pile with Stan's shirtsleeve and then closed the box. She wanted to justify the mess by informing her mother that she had been upstairs working at the computer all morning. She wasn't lazy. She wasn't dirty. She wasn't worthless. Instead she looked at Lena. "Sara is at a neighbor's, playing. Tell me about your doctor's appointment."

"Do you have a dishcloth—a *clean* one?" Her mother avoided the question with a question.

Shirley felt the muscles in her neck tighten. This tug-of-war was an all too familiar game they played. Shirley always lost.

Not this time. She took a deep breath and tried to

relax her tension. Then she handed her mother a fresh rag from the bottom drawer by the sink. "Have at it, Mom. Knock yourself out."

Fifteen minutes later, the kitchen was nearly clean, and Shirley and Lena had one more mother-daughter battle behind them.

"Why didn't you just tell me you were in town for your annual mammogram, Mom? Why did you have to worry me like that?"

"Worrying you is precisely what I was trying to avoid."

"Whatever."

"The first thing I told you was not to worry. Why are you on the defensive today, Shirley? You're not pregnant, are you?"

Shirley felt her neck muscles constrict again. "No. I'm not pregnant. Now, sit down."

"Excuse me?"

"Please, Mom. Have a seat. There is something I would like to talk to you about." Shirley decided there would never be a perfect time to get this validation thing under way, so she might as well take advantage of this time alone with her mother.

Lena rinsed the dishcloth and wiped the chair down while Shirley went to her bedroom. When she returned, she was carrying an envelope.

"What's this, a new diet?"

Shirley bit her lip until she could taste blood. "No, Mom. But it is going to help me get rid of some extra baggage." With that snappy comment Shirley suddenly realized she was on her own. Those $3.95 minutes had been a rip-off. No one had told Shirley *how* to seek validation.

"What is this—one of Sara's projects?"

"Nope. It's one of mine. It's my validation puzzle."

"Your what?" Lena sounded both confused and impatient. The way she always sounded when she wasn't so sure she had the upper hand.

"It's my attempt to feel validated by the people in my life who take me for granted. You know, I just want to feel acknowledged and appreciated."

"Don't we all?" Lena mumbled, but Shirley wasn't listening to anything except the pounding thunder of her own heart.

Shirley sat next to her mother at the now sparkling kitchen table and simply blurted out her deepest harbored feelings. She said something she had wanted to say to her mother ever since she was a child. "I hate buttermilk!"

Lena simply stared at her daughter for the longest minute of Shirley's life, then in that what's-wrong-with-you-now tone, she said, "Shirley, you're just having a very bad day."

The 1-900 number or not, she met her mother's gaze. "No, Mom. I'm actually having a pretty good day. Not an easy one, but a good one. There are just a few things I want you to know. Most of all, I love you. I really do. I know when Daddy walked out, you had to shoulder all of the responsibility of raising me. I don't pretend to know what that has been like for you, but I want you to know that I love you for it.

"I think we're a lot alike, Mom. But I am not you. I don't wash the dishes before I put them in the dishwasher. What's the point? I don't wear lipstick before noon. Okay, so there was that one time, but I'm not a high heels and ruby-red lips kind of woman. I buy my Thanksgiving rolls frozen in a plastic bag. I'm afraid of the sewing machine, Mom. Afraid of it, do you hear me?" Shirley had to pause to catch her breath.

Lena was no longer looking like a Supreme Court Justice, more like a distressed captive, eyeing the distance to the door. But Shirley was on a roll and couldn't allow herself to stop now.

"Mom, I'm very well aware of the fact that I'm overweight. You're not. I'm not a calorie counter like you. I think I'm more like one of those women who calories can count on. I'm fat and I know it, so there is no need for you to remind me every time we are together."

Another long and awkward pause seemed like it would never end. Then Shirley's mother asked quietly, "Is that it?"

"Did I mention that I detest buttermilk?"

"Yes, dear. You did."

"Okay, I guess that's it, then."

"My turn now?"

Shirley hesitated. "Fair's fair. Go for it, Mom."

"I love you, too. Really I do. More than you can

know. Sometimes I say the wrong things. Sometimes I do things that hurt you. I'm truly sorry for those times. It's just that we are so different—"

"Exactly!" agreed Shirley. "We're alike, but different. Mom, you are a walking tradition. I'm a tradition breaker."

"That's one of the things I like about you," confessed Shirley's mother.

Just hearing her mother pinpoint something she "liked" about her made Shirley feel good.

The next silence that followed was the longest one. But no words were needed as mother and daughter embraced in the most spontaneous hug they had ever experienced.

Shirley was positive she had finally broken through. Her mother loved her and accepted her for what she was. This validation stuff really was a breeze.

Shirley's mother was the first to back away from the hug. "May I ask you something while we are being so open with each other?"

"Sure, Mom." Shirley had not felt this close to her mother since she was ten years old. "Ask me anything." But even as she invited the query, she also braced herself. Conditioned response or instinct. Either way, Shirley's defenses went up.

"What's with all the 'S' names in your family?" Lena asked.

Shirley stared at her mother. "What's that supposed to mean?" She could feel a week's growth of hair on her legs and under her arms, bristling.

"Nothing. Nothing at all." Her mother backed down. "I've just wondered about the novelty of it and I've never dared ask before."

"So are you saying you don't like our kids' names?"

"No, that's not what I'm saying at all. I have just wondered, if your name was Zenith and Stan's name was Zeus, would all your kids have 'Z' names?"

"Maybe. Would that affect how you felt about them?"

"Shirley, you're ruining our bonding moment. You're being silly now. I was just curious, that's all. I'm sorry I offended you. But have you ever stopped to think that your mother might need, might even deserve, validation, too? I like to be included. Consulted, even. It's no fun making a child your whole life only to have that child grow up and exclude you from her adulthood."

"I'm sorry, Mom. I never knew you felt excluded. I am sorry." Shirley's apology was sincere.

They spent the next thirty minutes learning things about each other that neither had suspected. Then Sara came home and Grandma went out to watch her Rollerblade. Shirley finished the document that was due the next day. Then she dumped a can of soup over some skinless chicken breasts and popped them in the Crock-Pot. She even changed into real clothes and did a once-over on her face.

"Do you want to stay and have supper with us?" Shirley invited her mother.

"No, I don't think so. For some reason, I feel like that wrung-out dishrag of yours. I think I'll go home, fix a salad, and then have a shower and go to bed."

"Sounds like a great idea," said Shirley. "Except for the salad part," she joked.

"A salad or two might be good for—" Lena could not help herself.

Shirley put her finger on her lips and shook her head. "Shhh . . . shhh. Don't spoil this bonding moment."

So, what exactly had happened?, Shirley wondered. Now what was she supposed to do with that first piece of the puzzle? Had her mother actually validated her? Lena had acknowledged the fact that Shirley's feelings were justified; they'd even discussed the value of their diversity. But still, Shirley was a little unsure. It seemed there should be more. There was more. Maybe there was always more.

Validation does work both ways, Shirley was thinking when the telephone rang.

"Shirley, it's me, your mother."

"Hi, Mom. I recognized your voice."

"That's a good sign, I suppose. Anyway, listen to this. Yesterday when I got home I watched an *Oprah* episode, and guess what it was about?"

"Men who love women who are really men?"

"No, no. You've got Jenny Jones mixed up with

Oprah. Oprah has gone higher class now that she's got the power. Of course her ratings have dropped, but she doesn't do trash TV anymore."

"So what was the program about?"

"Validation! Can you believe it—validation!"

"No kidding?"

"I tried to tape it for you, but you know I still don't know how to push those two buttons on the VCR at once. I don't understand why you can't just push Record. It makes no sense, does it?"

"Life's complicated, Mom, but you're wandering. Tell me what Oprah had to say about validation."

"You'll have to watch the rerun, Shirley. I only caught part of it, but she said the same thing you said. We all need to be recognized for what we contribute. We need to feel appreciated. We need to feel like we matter."

"Amen."

"I've been thinking about something you said, Shirley. You and I are really not all that different."

Shirley smiled as she nestled the telephone receiver between her chin and shoulder so her hands were free to wipe the kitchen counters. The kitchen table was already clean. "I thought we established that yesterday, Mom. We have a lot of similarities, but also a lot of differences."

"Exactly." Lena sounded pleased. "We agree on more than you realize. I have a confession."

Shirley tossed the dishcloth into the sink and held

the receiver so she could hear clearly. "What kind of a confession, Mother?"

Lena laughed. "Nothing major. It's just that I hate buttermilk, too."

Shirley was shocked. "Then why on earth do you guzzle it by the quart? And why did you make me?"

"Because when I was a girl, my mother drank it and she made me. You don't know what gross is until you drink warm buttermilk. I guess you do what you get used to. But listen to this—I called my mother this morning and asked her, 'Why all the buttermilk?' You'll never guess what she said."

"So tell me."

"In her day and age, they didn't have electric refrigerators. They had iceboxes. I remember those iceboxes. Shirley, your generation is spoiled. You take it for granted that when you flip a switch a light will come on. When you want a cold drink, you open the fridge. It hasn't been that long ago that—"

"Mom, you're rambling."

"I'm sorry, dear. Where was I?"

"Buttermilk."

"Right." Lena paused long enough to gather her thoughts. "This open communication thing between us is so new, Shirley. You're just going to have to be patient with me if I get ahead of myself."

"No problem, Mom."

"Okay. Well, you know your grandmother, my mother, was raised on a farm. They milked their own cows morning and night. Nothing was wasted back then. The Great Depression, you know. So they had to hurry and drink the buttermilk they made before it spoiled. Turns out Mother hates the nasty stuff, too. It's just that her mother made her drink it and so she made me and I made you and don't you dare make Samantha or Sara."

"I couldn't even if I tried." Shirley laughed, feeling that the first piece of her puzzle now fit perfectly.

A few nights later, Shirley called Samantha, Sean, and Sara into her bedroom.

"Are we in trouble?" they wanted to know.

"No, but I think I might be."

It had been just another day in the life of Shirley. Up and at it before the rest of the family. Breakfast, two sack lunches, three batches of laundry, two loads to the dishwasher (Okay, so it was the same load twice—she forgot the soap the first time), a hunt for a missing school report on endangered panda bears, two trips to school and back, one to the bank, one to the dry cleaners, one to the grocery store. That was all before high noon. She had been right in the middle of designing a layout for a client when Sean called.

"Mom, I forgot to bring my stuffed panda to go along with my report. Please, can you bring it? Please?"

"Sure. Where is it?"

"It's in that big plastic sack where you shoved all

of our toys the day you were so mad. You were going to 'clean the house once and for all.' Remember?"

There had been so many "once and for alls" that Shirley did not remember. "I'll look for it, Sean," she promised weakly.

"Please, Mom. That's my oldest and most favorite toy. If I don't have it, my report will suck."

"Don't say suck. You know I hate that word."

"Sorry, Mom. I'll be watching for you from my classroom window."

She heard dial tone at about the same time she remembered that she had taken that sack of confiscated toys to Goodwill.

Half an hour later Shirley showed up at Sean's school with a stuffed toy.

"What's this?" Sean demanded.

"Isn't it your stuffed panda?" His mother feigned innocence.

"Mom! It's Sara's white dog! What did you do—color black spots on it with Magic Marker?"

Shirley shrugged her shoulders. "Shoe polish," she confessed. "I'm sorry, Son. I couldn't find your panda. I thought this would work."

"Well, it sucks."

Shirley shot him a mother's glare. She instinctively wanted to react the way she usually did, but just for that moment, she maintained control and was able to act instead of react. Her grimace slowly turned into a grin. "It does, doesn't it?"

That made Sean smile and he took the mutilated

mutt from his mother. "I'll try to explain to my class," he said, "but Sara is gonna kill you."

After school, there had been soccer practice, a piano lesson, a preschool parent-teacher conference, and of course she had attempted to run the stuffed dog through the washer. During the spin cycle, the machine had gotten off-balance and the dog came out gray, with all of its fake fur looking like the poor creature had been caught and frozen in an Arctic wind. In spite of her best efforts with hairstyling mousse and the blow dryer, the animal was in bad shape.

"What do you think?" she'd asked Sean.

He shook his head. "Now it looks more like a bear, Mom."

Oh, what a day! Somewhere in the middle of all of her "go-get-'em" was lodged a lot of guilt. She had started with the best of intentions. Half a bagel—no cream cheese. Two of her eight required daily glasses of water. There had been a glimmer of hope sometime during the morning. There was always the promise she made to herself to exercise— "Just as soon as I have a break."

A mad dash around the neighborhood *had* managed to accelerate her heart rate. The family dog was in heat and the little tramp had decided to go socializing. Shirley finally found her down the block in a garage with a Doberman. She had somehow managed to pry them apart and dragged the whimpering dachshund home. She immediately locked her in the bathroom.

The entire episode left Shirley famished and all she could find was a leftover chocolate-glazed donut. Of course, she felt guilty for gobbling it, but there wasn't time for guilt. Not at the moment. Let it build. She could bask in it later.

Stan called and ask her to pick up a part for the family boat, which had not been on the water in years. Oh, and if she wasn't doing anything else, could she gas up the car and run it through the wash?

When Shirley picked Sara up from preschool the poor child had been starving, so out of concern and compassion (not to mention guilt for the stuffed dog, although Sara had been forgiving), Shirley took her to McDonald's for a Happy Meal.

Shirley could not be rude to the man at the drive-up window who asked, "Would you care to try one of our combo meals today?"

"Sure."

"Would you like that super-sized for a small additional fee?"

She hesitated. Then she looked at the guy. He could not have been more than sixteen. Maybe this was his first day on the job. How could she say no?

She couldn't.

After a Big Mac attack came another wave of guilt. Guilt could wait. Guilt could always wait.

There was shopping to do, dinner to prepare, envelopes that needed to be stuffed for the PTA. The phone rang thirteen times. Four were wrong numbers. Three were generated by computerized salespeople. Twice, Shirley's mother had called.

"Shirley, we're finally bonding! Oprah said this might take some time."

There were more dirty dishes. A broken pipe. Sara wanted to make a horse stable out of Popsicle sticks, so she took everything out of the freezer to thaw. Sean needed a new pair of shoes—by soccer practice tomorrow morning. Samantha was in a fight with her best friend, so she needed Shirley's consolation.

Stan did call—to say he was working late and would not be home for dinner.

The doorbell rang for the seventeenth time. It was the little neighbor boy. "Can Sara play?" he asked for the seventeenth time that day.

Shirley loved her family. Her husband and children meant everything to her. It's just that she felt overwhelmed and under-appreciated at times. They expected so much from her. They needed so much. They deserved so much.

But there was only so much Shirley had to give. There were times she thought of getting in the car and driving away. She could never abandon them, but this mothering business was a full-time occupation. There were no breaks. No paid vacations. She was always on call.

It was about time they started validating her feelings, her needs, and her contributions to their lives. If they weren't sure just exactly what those contributions were, Shirley was prepared to clarify.

Now she sat on the bed next to her kids.

"What's wrong, Mom?" Samantha wanted to know.

Shirley was not certain where to begin. "You kids know how much I love you, don't you?"

"Yeah," they responded in unison.

"How do you show people that you love them?" she asked.

Sara raised her hand and shouted at the same time. "You hug them!"

Shirley rumpled her daughter's preschool curls. "Good, honey."

"You do stuff for them," answered Sean.

Shirley smiled wearily. "What do I do for you kids that shows how much I love you?"

Samantha didn't hesitate. "You listen to us."

"You come to watch my soccer games," said Sean, "even when the coach won't let me play."

"You read stories to me and do all of those funny voices," Sara added.

This wasn't at all what Shirley had expected or prepared for. Her defenses were up, but they obviously didn't need to be. Still, she wondered if she was getting through to her children.

"What about all of the big home-cooked meals I make for you?"

"I like the way you put cinnamon and sugar on toast," said Sean.

Samantha reached over and put her hand on Shirley's. "Me, too. What is this all about, Mom—for real?"

Shirley didn't want to lose her direction. "What about the way I clean the house for you?"

Samantha and Sean looked at each other with uncertainty, but Sara didn't hesitate. "I thought that lady who comes here every week cleans the house."

"Well, she doesn't," stated Shirley defensively. "And she only comes every *other* week to help me stay on top of the details. I do almost all of the work."

"I clean my room," said Sean.

"So do I," said Samantha.

"You do not!" Sean contested.

"Well, your room is a pigsty. Mom says she needs a shot before she even dares to walk in your room!"

Shirley listened to the banter and pictured herself "needing a shot" before she ventured into the chaos of her children's rooms. Vodka was the kind of "shot" she allowed herself to envision. The thought made her smile because things were not nearly that bad. "It was a joke, Sami. I was talking about a tetanus shot."

"See, I told you!" Samantha yelled. "You're a pig, Sean!"

"I am not! You are!" he shouted back.

Shirley could feel the situation quickly turning against her. "Whatever! Just look at me and listen to me for a minute—please. All I am asking for is your honest opinion. Do you realize how hard I work for this family?" She knew she was begging, but these were her offspring, the bone of her bone, the flesh of her flesh. If she could not bare her soul to them, there was no safe place in her existence.

"Mom, you're whining."

"I know I am, Sami. Sometimes even moms deserve a good whine now and then."

"So where is this thing going?"

"You are almost a teenager, aren't you?" she mused. "One day you'll see how much work goes into running this house, this family, and maybe then you'll appreciate me."

Samantha looked straight at her mother. "We appreciate you, Mom. We know how hard you work for us."

Sara snuggled over and jostled herself into Shirley's lap. "You're a yummy cook, Mommy. We love your dinners."

"We love your dinners and the house always looks nice," Samantha agreed, "but sometimes . . . " She looked at Sean, her eyes pleading for support. "Sometimes after you cook and clean you are so tired and so . . . "

"Grumpy!" her brother finished her thought. "That's why we love hot-dog nights. You always have time to play Monopoly and baseball and stuff with us."

Shirley gripped Sara for support. "You love hot dogs better than my French Chicken Spinach in Pastry?"

They all nodded their confession.

"We even like cold-cereal nights when Daddy tends us because after we eat he plays video games with us."

"Cold cereal and hot dogs, huh? I'm dumb-founded."

Sara twisted her little body so she could look her mother directly in the eyes. "No, you're not dumb, Mommy. Just wrong about the chicken."

It was a good thing it was Friday night because everyone stayed up way past their bedtimes. Talking. Learning. Cuddling. Laughing. Recognizing and appreciating what each one contributed to the family.

No one mentioned the shiny kitchen floor or the way Shirley cleaned deep into the corners with an old toothbrush. No one mentioned the sparkling toilet bowls on which she used the same old toothbrush to scrub all those hard-to-reach places.

No, Shirley and her children talked about the little adventures that the family went on together. They all remembered the day Shirley made a home-made slide out of a piece of painter's heavy-duty plastic and the garden hose. They didn't mention the expensive fancy holiday outfits that Shirley had worked and scrimped and saved for. They remembered the tie-dyed T-shirts they made together in the sink one afternoon.

Shirley learned more about herself and her children that night than she could have in a lifetime of professional parenting courses.

This was a time to replenish her empty soul, to rejuvenate her wilting spirit. This was a time to give and to get. This was Shirley's night to be on the receiving end.

Her kids weren't the ones who imposed so many demands on her. Shirley did that to herself. Of course, they did require a great deal of her time and energy, but they cherished her. Their mom. Not just the things she did for them.

They didn't need anything fancy, elaborate or expensive. Shirley was smart enough to appreciate that while it lasted; those teenage years would soon be upon them. Her children needed her. Her time. Her energy. Her love. In spite of all of her misgivings, Samantha, Sean, and Sara did appreciate their mother.

Shirley suddenly felt overwhelmed with peace and contentment. Three more pieces of her puzzle were complete. At least for tonight, anyway.

"I love you because you feed my dog when I forget to," said Sean.

"I love you because you take me to the mall and listen to me talk about all my friends," said Samantha.

"I love you because you gave my dog a cool hairdo. And you took me to McDonald's and then we had a picnic on the lawn," Sara said.

Reality returned.

"You took Sara to McDonald's and not us!" the other two children screamed their protest.

*   *   *

When Stan came home sometime around midnight he found his wife and children all cuddled on the master bed, sleeping soundly. It looked to him like they had been having one heck of a party— catered by McDonald's.

The puzzle was taking shape—one piece at a time. Slowly, but steadily. Whenever she felt a particular piece represented validation, Shirley would carefully glue it onto a sturdy matte board. She intended to have it professionally framed when the last piece was complete. It was a work of art that deserved a prominent spot in her heart as well as her house. She wanted to be able to look at it often, as sort of a validation reminder or renewal. She would have to hang it in just the right spot . . . most likely the bathroom.

In the meantime, Shirley's former boss was too much on her mind. His was a piece of the puzzle Shirley didn't even want to touch. Why had she ever included him in her life again? That chapter had been finished. Or at least it would be, once and for all, by the end of the afternoon. She had an appointment to return to campus to meet with the man who had brought so much conflict and confusion to her life. So much pain.

As she fingered his piece of the puzzle, it was not only darker, its edges were jagged, like daggers or shards of glass. She couldn't help thinking that the man might still be dangerous. Maybe she should call and cancel the appointment. No, if she could face Lena, she could face him.

Shirley had landed her first real job during her senior year of college. As the personal aid to the dean of psychology, she was under the impression that she had received a lucky break. Shirley was considering a career in counseling back then, and she viewed this as a tremendous opportunity to learn from a brilliant man whom everyone so respected and admired. Even her mother had applauded Shirley's coup. "Maybe I can get some free therapy for a change," she'd half-joked with her daughter. "Heaven knows I've shelled out enough money to therapists to pay for an entire psychology building."

During that first month of employment, the only therapy Shirley practiced was on the lab rats as she fed them, weighed them, and cleaned their cages. She also graded students' tests and filed papers. This wasn't the work she had signed on for, but she was willing to pay her dues and a little extra.

She organized the office. Arranged the dean's schedule. She even came in early so she could have his steaming black coffee ready when he arrived. This was her golden opportunity and she was determined to make the most of it.

By the end of that first month, the man who could lecture for hours on the human condition had never once called Shirley by name. He had not thanked her or even acknowledged her presence, except to leave notes chiding her when her work did not meet his expectations.

So he's reserved, she told herself.

She could deal with that.

So he's distant, she excused him six months later. At least now he was criticizing her to her face.

"Are you sure you're not just substituting this man for your absentee father?" Shirley's mother had inquired of her. "It won't work, you know."

"Mom, I'm the psychology major, remember?" That was the last time Shirley confided her frustrations to her mother.

Stan was the one who provided a shoulder to cry on, and if Shirley remembered correctly, that was about the time he offered more than just a shoulder.

Shirley wore her diamond engagement ring with pride. Her life was a happy one, all except for the job that had now become their only source of income, since Stan was wrapping up his senior year as well.

A year into the job, Shirley excused her boss's deteriorating conduct by attributing it to his abundant intellect and her lack of intelligence.

The dean was superior.

She was inferior.

"Why don't you just quit the job?" Stan asked her over and over. "There are other jobs."

"Then why don't you get one?" she snapped at him one evening.

He did. Stan landed a job on a road construction crew, and between his studies and his work, Shirley hardly ever saw the man that was not only her fiancé, but the best friend of her life.

It was on a weekend when Stan was away that the

dean began paying attention to Shirley. He had actually invited her to show him the grant proposal she had been working on since her graduation.

Shirley had been flattered and excited. It was a project that would propel her toward her master's degree, bring a great deal of money to the school, and help children in nccd.

"Come by Saturday evening," the dean said. "We'll have time to go over it without any interruptions."

Shirley had polished it all day Saturday and had it waiting on his desk when the dean arrived. He glanced at it and then looked up at Shirley who was trying not to look too anxious.

"Have a seat," he invited, pulling a chair alongside his.

Shirley sat down slowly, unsure.

"You are a very attractive young woman," the dean said unexpectedly. Then he reached over and laid his hand on her knee.

For an entire year, she had been desperate for this man to acknowledge her. To speak to her. To make direct eye contact with her. But now that his hand was on her leg, she cringed under his touch. She stiffened and he moved away. That was not the last time he had reached for her during that weekend.

When Stan got home on Sunday evening, Shirley was sitting outside of his dormitory waiting for him. "What's wrong, babe?" he asked her as he took

Shirley into his arms. It was the only place in her world where she felt totally secure.

She intended to tell him, but the words would not come. After all, nothing had actually happened. Had it? Maybe Shirley was just overreacting. She had a tendency to do that. "Nothing," she finally said. "I just missed you more than you can know."

Weeks went by and Shirley did her best to avoid spending any time alone with the dean, whose sudden interest in her, Shirley deemed inappropriate at best. She worked on the grant proposal at the library, and when it was completed, she felt certain the school would receive the requested funding. It was a pet project of hers—a counseling shelter for children of domestic violence. Not only would the children receive help, but the program would provide assistance for the families in crisis.

Shirley was very proud of the project and submitted it to the dean with confidence, making certain she maintained a professional distance.

"I'm very excited about this," she admitted.

"I'll read it late this evening. Why don't you stop by the office about ten-thirty and we'll talk about it?"

"I'm sorry. I can't tonight," she lied.

"It could mean a big difference in its acceptance or rejection."

"I don't understand."

"A grant proposal requires attention to specifics. I've noticed that in the other proposals you've written for me, you tend to be too general. Too broad."

He laughed viciously, as if he were the only one on an inside joke. "I could give you some of the details you're lacking."

"I'm sorry, not tonight."

Shirley waited until past midnight and then she had a roommate walk with her to the psychology building, where they made sure the lights were out, and the office was empty before they entered. That's when Shirley discovered that the dean had read her proposal, approved of it, had removed the cover sheet with her name, and had replaced it with *only* his own name and credentials.

Her roommate had asked repeatedly why Shirley was so upset. Shirley had remained quiet and never disclosed the betrayal she felt, not even to those closest to her. Not even to Stan. He would have made her face the man and that was not something Shirley felt ready for. Stan would have made a scene. A scene would have caused humiliation and Shirley thought her way was the best way. The quiet conqueror. A silent victory. Sans confrontation.

The next morning Shirley had intended to confront the dean, but he had reverted back to his cold, distant, critical self. "I read your proposal. It has potential, but it's not worth the work. The project itself lacks merit."

"Merit?" Shirley had wanted to rant and rave. To scratch the man across his twisted face. She was standing in front of both Jekyll and Hyde. The creep. The pervert. The loser. No, loser would be her. Shirley did nothing. She remained silent and let the dean take all of the credit.

When the proposal was eventually accepted and the school received the grant money, the dean claimed it was because he had rewritten the entire project and had made it his own.

"You could have at least mentioned me in your speech," she managed.

It was the first time he ever called her by her name. "Shirley, you're mistaken."

Why she stayed on after that only supported his observation. She *was* dumb.

When the dean finally fired her, he did it by moving his office across campus—without telling her. Shirley showed up for work one Monday morning and the janitor informed her. "That guy has been promoted to administration. These past couple of years, he's really shined. He's worked hard for his new post. Do you know he landed a million-dollar government contract to help kids?"

Shirley nodded. "She didn't trust her voice because her throat felt like she had suddenly swallowed a Brillo pad.

Stan had warned her. Told her to stand up to the guy. Her friends had warned her. Told her to turn him in. Raise a stink. Even her mother had told her to look for a new job. Shirley had ignored them all and had stayed until leaving was no longer her choice.

When she finally tracked the good professor down, and was granted the privilege of a one-on-one, it was only because he was coming down a narrow hallway and there was no place to retreat.

"I'm sorry, sir. I don't understand. Why wasn't I informed of this move?"

He did not look at her; he hadn't looked at her since she had given him the proposal. "Shirley, you can't be surprised. My career is now headed in a different direction. Administration is providing me with a pool of secretarial assistants. There will not be a position for you here. See the personnel office for your final paycheck."

With that, he walked past her, brushing his body against hers until she shuddered at his touch. Then he was gone, and so was any shred of self-confidence she had.

He was the most intellectual man Shirley had ever known. This was the man whose respect she had spent nearly two years trying desperately to earn. Two years!

This was the man who had taught her her place as a subordinate.

This was the man whose shadow still darkened her thoughts and gave her nightmares.

Now Shirley sat in his worn, but plush executive office, waiting for her scheduled ten-minute appointment. The dean had left the college and was now employed with a corporation.

It had been a decade and a half since Shirley had

been left standing in that narrow hallway, unable to breathe for a very long time, unable to walk away. Once she did, she thought she would never look back, but now she found herself looking back into those beady eyes.

"Am I supposed to know you?" he asked as he walked into the room.

He was old now. Hunched and frail looking. His voice was raspy, but his condescending demeanor had not changed. Those old feelings of inferiority overwhelmed Shirley, but only momentarily.

Shirley extended her hand to him and introduced herself, making sure she emphasized her maiden name. He sat down at his desk without extending his own hand to her.

"What is it that you want?"

"Well . . . Sir . . . " she stammered. This was not going to be easy. "I would like to tell you how I feel about the way I was treated whcn I was your assistant at the psychology department."

His eyes narrowed suspiciously. Then she could tell he recognized her, although his expression did not vary. "Was there a problem?" he asked, sounding less confident than Shirley remembered.

"As a matter of fact . . . "

Shirley knew time was short, so she did not waste a minute. She got right to the core, pouring out her heart, telling him how much her job had meant to her, how hard she had worked for him. How betrayed she felt by him.

"I did a good job for you, sir. Better than good. I wrote that grant and you took all of the credit. There were other times when your behavior toward me was inappropriate."

He attempted to sit erect, then leaned toward her, narrowing his eyes until they were only dark slits.

Shirley swallowed hard. She could feel that old Brillo pad scratching at her throat. "Sir, I didn't say anything then because I felt inferior. Insecure. Afraid. Well, I'm not afraid anymore."

He attempted to clear his own throat. "There is a statute of limitations on these matters," he said firmly. "I know."

Shirley shifted backward. What had just happened? The old man had revealed his true self. She spent her last minute just letting the weight of the moment shift from her shoulders to his.

Then Shirley stood and stared down at the little man. She looked at him and waited until he lifted his slits to meet her gaze.

"You don't get it, do you? You might be intelligent, but you're not a very smart man. Intellect will never replace integrity. Good-bye, Professor."

This time he was the one left alone.

Shirley glanced back one more time, just for a reality check, because the whole experience seemed sort of surreal. Everything from his shriveled appearance, to her commanding tone, and the things that had come out of her mouth! Who was this powerhouse in her body?

She stopped to stare through the partially open door at the end of the hallway. There sat the professor, the dean, the academic genius. He was all those things and probably more. But for now, she saw his true side; he was just a little man behind a big desk. The intellectual giant himself. The professor of the human psyche. Was it Shirley's imagination . . . or was the shrink shrinking?

When Shirley got out to her car, she ripped that "dark" piece of her validation puzzle into confetti.

Why that man ever had any power over the way she felt about herself, Shirley could not imagine now. Her mistake. A giant mistake, but all hers.

It was also a mistake to think that she needed his validation. He just wasn't worth it. Stan always said that "what goes around comes around." She had never fully appreciated that saying until now. In spite of her better self, Shirley could not help but feel a little validation from the fact that the old professor had obviously gotten some of what was due him.

She now realized that she was the one who had given him power, and taking it back was all of the validation she needed.

It had been an eternity since Shirley's high-school days. Mrs. Montgomery was about retirement age then, so Shirley wasn't exactly sure how she was going to track her down now.

One long-distance phone call to Franklin High

and she discovered a search wasn't going to be necessary.

"I'm sorry, but Mrs. Montgomery passed away several years ago," Shirley was informed.

Late that night when the only sound in the house was the clothes dryer down the hallway turning and turning, Shirley was lying in bed, thoughts of Mrs. Montgomery turning in her head.

A load of jeans was set for the "less dry" cycle, and with each turn, the copper rivets hit against the metal barrel of the dryer. Actually, Shirley liked the rhythmic sound. She wished the cycle in her head could be as soothing.

Times like these provided Shirley some of her most peaceful moments. With Stan snoring every once in a while next to her, and the kids all slumbering soundly in their bedrooms, Shirley felt surrounded by soft security.

She reached up and turned on the lamp next to her. Stan grunted. "The light's right in my eyes."

"Turn over." She rolled his torso away from her and pulled the quilt up around his shoulder. "Go back to sleep. I'm going to be awake for a while."

"What are you doing?"

"A puzzle."

"You're putting a puzzle together at this time of night?"

"I am."

"Why don't you just read one of your magazines for women? That should put you to sleep."

"Very funny."

She scratched his back in giant circles until Stan went back to sleep. It took about thirty seconds.

In the nightstand next to her bed was a large manila envelope. She unclasped it and dumped the contents out on the bedcovers in front of her. There was the matte board with several of the validation puzzle pieces glued in place. There were a couple of other envelopes, one with the professor's sprinkling of shredded paper and one with the remaining pieces of the puzzle. There was also an English report that Shirley had kept tucked away for more years than she cared to count.

Shirley sorted out Mrs. Montgomery's piece and then picked up the English report. She recalled how hard she had worked on that report. Chaucer was no easy subject, but she had tackled the early author to please and impress Mrs. Montgomery.

Shirley had accomplished neither.

Right now she could not help but compare her efforts to please Mrs. Montgomery to all of the work she had put in to win her psychology professor's admiration. There were a lot of similarities between the two experiences, and Shirley hoped that a pattern wasn't emerging. Okay, so she was a people-pleaser. Big deal.

She looked carefully at the report. It wasn't the C grade that had whittled away at Shirley for all of these years. It was the judgment, written in Mrs. Montgomery's own hand.

"There is no shame in being average."

Average. Ordinary. Plain. Stupid.

Shirley was not just a C student; she was a C human being.

Up until that moment, Shirley had lived her young life believing that she was rather special. Different. Unique. Filled with potential. She knew she seldom met her mother's expectations, but Shirley still felt she was someone with a future. Then Mrs. Montgomery passed that report from student to student until it reached the back of the room where Shirley sat in Advanced English Literature.

One comment had changed her entire perspective of herself.

After that, it didn't matter how many other teachers gave her A's and B's and said, "Shirley, you have tremendous talent and potential."

No. Shirley was average.

Maybe that's why she had endured the "good" professor's abuse for so long during college.

Maybe that's why it had taken her all these years to stand up for herself.

Mrs. Montgomery had been wrong. There was great shame in being average.

Now, for the first time since Shirley had read that remark, she could see the devastating impact it had had on her adult life.

It had labeled her.

She had worn that label with shame. More importantly, she had believed that label, and because she had believed that she was nothing special, she had treated herself as nothing special.

Clearly, it had been evident during her tenure with the professor. It was clear in her relationship with her family, particularly her mother. No matter what her mother meant, Shirley always interpreted her comments as some way of saying, "You are a disappointment to me."

In the farthest and darkest corners of her mind, maybe she even believed her father had abandoned Shirley and her mother because Shirley was average—an inadequate daughter. Whenever she allowed herself to think about her father, Shirley would squeeze her eyes so tightly that she gave herself a headache. Right now, she could feel a whopper coming on.

In spite of all that was average about Shirley and her life, there was no way to deny those moments of absolute glory that were anything but ordinary. Like the night that Stan had proposed. And what could compare to those three magical moments when her body had produced two daughters and a son? She had been in full partnership with The Miracle Maker. There was no euphoria like the one produced by new motherhood. Of course, she knew that had a great deal to do with the invention of the epidural, but so what? A high like that was a high like no other.

It was nights like tonight that Shirley wondered what would fill her life if she did not have Stan and the children. Where would she be if fate had not granted her this family? The thought made her shift uncomfortably, and one of the pieces of her puzzle fell to the floor. She reached over and gently placed Mrs. Montgomery's name back on her lap. She had learned much from this validation process; but there was still so much to learn.

She was not just a mere extension of her family. No. She was the hub of the home; beyond that, she was an individual. She had to be able to stand on her own before she could stand with Stan and the children as a member of the family. "Strong individuals make strong families"—where had she heard that thought? She could not recall, but decided it was one she would type up and post by her computer where she always placed thoughts to inspire her.

Shirley wanted to be strong. She told herself she was. She was a bright, witty, warm, and at times, insightful woman. During this silent midnight pep talk Shirley did not feel average. Hardly. Then came the immediate and familiar doubts, marching into her thoughts like robbers, ready to steal any sign of self-confidence. She engaged in one fleeting moment of uncertainty, but then forced herself to pick up the pen. As she did, her self-doubts disappeared and she began to write.

Dear Mrs. Montgomery,

You were the most influential teacher of my education, at least until now. I admired you, respected you, and hoped to emulate you.

I don't know why I do that—latch on to cer-

tain people and allow them power to influence me. I suppose that means there is a void in my life that needs filling. I certainly opened my porous soul to you and allowed you carte blanche. When you labeled me as "average," I should have talked to you face-to-face. But after that, I don't believe I was ever able to make eye contact with you again.

If you were standing in front of me tonight, Mrs. Montgomery, I would look you directly in the eye. I would tell you that you were wrong. I am not average. In fact, I've never met an average person in my life. By God's own design, we are all unique individuals, with gifts to offer life and ways of giving that set us apart from one another. You were a teacher. You taught school for thirty years. You should have known that.

Today I feel extremely successful. I am well into the second decade of marriage to a man whom I adore. I am the mother of three great kids, none of whom is average. I have friends. I have faith.

I own my own business. People pay me for my skills. I am ever learning.

I am blessed.

In your eyes, my life might not amount to much; I may be just average. But Mrs. Montgomery, I'm not looking through your eyes anymore.

"Yes!" Shirley shouted out loud as she finished the letter. "Yes! Yes! Yes!"

"Turn off the light," grumbled Stan. "What are you doing, anyway?"

"Writing a letter."

"A letter? Who are you writing to in the middle of the night?"

"To a dead woman."

Stan rolled onto his stomach and buried his face in the pillow. "Shirley, you're crazy," he yawned. "Surely . . . you are."

Shirley folded the letter and put it in the manila envelope with all of her other validation paraphernalia. Then she clasped it tightly. She was slowly realizing how precious every single piece was.

Tomorrow she would glue another piece of the puzzle in place. For now, the clothes dryer had stopped; she had to get up and hang those jeans just right so they could finish drying and gravity would save her the task of ironing them.

Such an ordinary chore for such an extraordinary woman, she thought, and then allowed that thought to linger.

"I really am tired," she chuckled into the stillness of the night.

The list was dwindling. Every few days, another piece of the puzzle fit, or at least came close. Shirley was feeling the *wholeness* of the experience. Would it ever be truly complete?

Shoved back into those crammed and dark recesses of her mind were thoughts about her father. Why wasn't his name on her list? Why didn't he have a piece of her puzzle?

She didn't need his validation. She didn't need anything from him. The man had walked out and never looked back. As a child, she had learned to live without him. She would live through this without him, too. Besides, if Lena ever found out Shirley was in contact with her father, she would find herself motherless.

Validation wasn't what was needed here. It wasn't as if there was an empty void waiting to be filled. No, that void was filled with other things—like resentment, hate, fear, pain, and the big one—the question, "Why?"

Shirley also wondered about another father. Why hadn't she given God a piece of her puzzle? She was a woman of deep faith. She believed in heaven. She believed in angels. She believed in God. So when she had been making a list of the people who were most important in her life, why had she excluded God from it?

She didn't know His phone number, for one thing. Besides, God was busy. The world was in crisis. Who was Shirley to think that she could get through to the Source of All Life? Even if she did try, she was convinced the number would be busy.

If the line was free, then what? What if *He* answered? What would she say?

"Hello, God. It's me, Shirley. Um . . . I've got this validation thing going on. Of course, you already know that because you know everything. You're God. Anyway, I'm sorry to bother you, but I was wondering if you could answer a few questions for me. Are you real? Do you exist? Where did you come from? Where is heaven? Why am I here? Do I have a destiny? Am I fulfilling it? If you were going to grade me, would you give me a 'C'? 'C' means average, you know. I don't think I'm average, do you? Why is there so much hate and pain and suffering in this world? Will it be worth it in the end? And what exactly is the 'end'? Is there life after death? What will it be like? Where's my dad? Why did he leave us? Was it my fault? Is my marriage going to last or is Stan going to walk out one day? What's wrong with me?

"I'm sorry to ramble; I have a tendency to do that. I get it from my mother. You know my mother, don't you, God? Lena talks to you all the time. I think she's mad at you. I'm not mad at you. Are you mad at me?"

The conversation that was playing in her head was so one-sided that Shirley had to wonder, if she did get through to God, would He be able to get a word in edgewise? What if she was granted an audience with The Almighty, and allowed only one question—what would it be?

Ah . . . she would think about that later. Right now, her puzzle was coming together and she didn't want to let doubts dance on her merriment.

Even though the process seemed simplistic, perhaps juvenile, it was working. She could feel it. She was getting to know herself better than she ever had. More importantly, she liked herself better than she ever had.

One morning, Shirley decided it was time for a new hair appointment. Whenever she let her hair go too long, she imagined that it started to look like her mother's. There were some things she wanted to emulate about her mother; hairstyle was not one of them. The kids called it "Grandma's football helmet hair."

Shirley figured that as long as she was making so many changes in her life, she might as well approach everything with confidence.

She washed and dried and styled her hair.

Stan eyed her suspiciously. "I thought you were on your way to a hair appointment."

"I am."

"Then why did you just fix your own hair?"

"I can't walk in there and let them see me with it all ratty, can I?"

"I thought that was the whole idea. You go in looking bad and come out looking good. Isn't that why you fork over the big bucks?"

"What are you saying, that I look bad?"

He held both palms up in defense. "Nope. You look great, hon." Then from behind his newspaper shield, she heard him snicker, "As long as you like helmet hair."

"Funny, Mr. Clean," she said, brushing her hand over his receding hairline.

"You think I'm going bald, don't you?" he asked, revealing his own insecurity.

"No, Stanley. Not at all. If anything, your hair is thicker and your waistline thinner than the day I married you."

"I thought so," was all he said before turning back to his newspaper.

Oblivion could be sweet, she thought, if only she could retreat into it every once in a while. Not Shirley. No. She had to be aware of every blissful or painful or annoying detail surrounding her. Shirley couldn't help believing that there were no "little things" and no "little people." Everything and everyone mattered. There were so many times when she wished that she could be more like Stan. He didn't let things or people get to him the way that she did, but Shirley was not Stan.

For some reason, the significant people on her puzzle list had been easier, in a way, than the casual acquaintances. It made sense that Shirley wanted and needed validation from her mother. It was perfectly reasonable that she wanted to set the record straight with her former boss. Her husband and children had to be the most critical pieces of her puzzle. Friends were logical pieces to her validation puzzle. Even some of her neighbors had small pieces. Those choices made sense.

But her hairstylist? The milkman? The girl she hired to help with the housework? Why Shirley sought validation from them, she wasn't sure—but she did.

Shirley had a standing appointment with Debbie every few months. A cut and style was typical, but there were also the "highlights," "streaks," or "dye jobs" that her stubborn roots required on a regular basis. She used to get "perms" every once in a while, and liked the lift they gave to her limp hair, but Debbie told her last time that "perms" were out. Frizz was never really in.

Debbie was young—twenty-two at the most. Single. Skinny, skinny. Adorable. She had perfect long, thick shiny hair. The kind Shirley would have killed for. Straight white teeth about which any orthodontist would have been proud to say, "That smile is my work."

Debbie smiled a lot. In fact, she laughed out loud at Shirley's jokes. No wonder Shirley liked her so much.

Debbie was up on every style and fashion change. She knew every obscure music group, especially the ones that were now deemed "alternative." After spending a couple of hours with Debbie, Shirley came home and could actually start a conversation that would capture Samantha's attention.

"How about those Walking Zombies?"

"Wow, Mom. Where do you learn these things?"

"I like to keep up."

"Then you'd know they aren't 'The Walking Zombies' but 'The Hungry Zombies.' "

"Oh, okay. Whatever."

"How about letting me show you their latest CD? It's on sale at the mall."

Samantha lived to go to the mall. Shirley would rather be sprayed with Mace.

"Maybe when your father comes home we can all go."

"That's not cool, Mom. My friends will think I'm baby-sitting."

About this time, Shirley would realize how fast her daughter was growing up. The parent pressure was giving way to the peer pressure.

"Okay, when Dad gets home, he can tend and I'll take you to the mall. Can you stand to be seen with your mother?"

"Can we buy that CD?"

At this point Shirley would realize that a little information could be a very dangerous thing indeed. "The Hungry Zombies—are they that new rock and roll band who wrap themselves in bloody bandages?"

"No, Mom. Those are The Walking Mummies. Get with it."

"I am with it."

"You're bogus. You've been talking to Debbie again, haven't you?"

This is where Shirley would confess that she wasn't "hip" or "happenin' "—just a mother anxious to stay in touch with her daughter.

"Maybe we should invite Debbie to go to the mall with us," Samantha would say, only half-teasing.

Debbie was not actually a friend, but an acquaintance that Shirley valued. She had provided Shirley with enough information to open the lines of communication with Samantha, and Debbie always made Shirley feel good. Still, there were a few things about Debbie that drove Shirley crazy. For one thing, the girl wore heels eight hours a day and never complained. Shirley couldn't wear heels that high to a funeral without having to take them off underneath the pew.

For another thing, Debbie always wore Shirley's favorite color—black. On Shirley it seemed to scream that she was trying to hide something that was too big to be hidden. On Debbie it accentuated all the right parts. And Debbie had plenty of those. Her black jumpsuits, hot pants and mini-skirts verified that. She kept a roll of masking tape at her styling station. She wrapped the tape around her hand, with the sticky side out, so she could keep her outfits hair-free and looking perfect.

Everything about Debbie seemed a little too perfect. She was one of those perfect people that Shirley wanted to prejudge and to hate, but just could not because Debbie was so nice. Maybe that's why Shirley cared so much about what Debbie thought of her. She was living Shirley's fantasy youth.

"Hi, Shirley," Debbie squeaked her usual enthusiastic greeting. "What are we doing today?"

Debbie was wearing black stretch pants, a white cotton T-shirt, and a black vest. No bra. Everything about Debbie was, well . . . perky.

Black heels, too. High and spiky. Her hair was done in some fancy French braid and her earrings matched her hair clip. Shirley felt very old and very frumpy in her baggy gray jogging suit and old scuffed Nikes.

Once, when Stan had suggested that he visit Debbie for a haircut, Shirley had objected. Now she realized why.

"Are you okay, Shirley?" Debbie asked. "You seem a little down."

"I'm okay."

"What are we doing today?" Debbie repeated.

"The usual," Shirley replied, but then surprised herself with a change of mind. "No, I want something different. Something that doesn't remind me of my mother. Something that is hip and hop and happenin'."

"You go, girl." Debbie laughed. "How about something a little on the sassy side?"

"Sounds good to me."

Following their usual exchange of pleasantries—music, clothes, kids, and an update on Debbie's ever-exciting love life, Shirley decided to launch right in.

"I really admire you, Debbie."

Debbie seemed surprised. "You admire me—why?"

"You are always so happy. So pulled together. So beautiful and talented. You spend eight hours a day helping people to feel better about themselves."

Debbie was standing in back of Shirley, but Shirley could see the girl's expression in the mirror. Debbie was deeply touched by the comment.

"No one has ever said anything like that to me."

"You're kidding."

Debbie raised the scissors and began clipping. "No. People are always very nice, just not very deep."

Shirley thought about that while Debbie clipped and snipped. She thought how disgusted someone like Debbie must be with Shirley for letting herself go. Her no-style hair, her excess weight, her lack of makeup, her oversized and boring wardrobe, her stay-put lifestyle. She was just about to justify it all to the woman who did her hair when Debbie broke Shirley's concentration.

"You're the one *I* admire, Shirley."

Now it was Shirley's expression that registered surprise. "Me? Why on earth would you say such a thing?"

"Because it's true. I admire you. I have since the first day I met you."

"Me?" was all Shirley could manage to repeat.

"You amaze me, Shirley. You are a wife and a mother. You always talk about your family with such love. Most women come in here and sit and complain about their husbands and children. You just talk about how much you love them."

"Stan and the kids are great."

"See . . . that's exactly what I mean. You build them up. You should be the poster woman for the next millennium. You have your own business. You are funny and smart. Every time you come in, I learn something new from you. You have always just read some great book. You talk to people. You care about how you look, but you go so much deeper than appearances."

Shirley could not believe this young girl's observations. "Don't stop now," she joked.

Debbie grinned and spun the styling chair around so that the two women were facing each other. "Shirley, I always look forward to your appointments because I feel better about myself after you've been here."

There was no doubting Debbie's sincerity or Shirley's shock at the compliment.

Once again, Shirley had been wrong. There was no need to seek Debbie's validation—she already had it.

"What do you think of your new hairstyle?" Debbie asked, spinning the chair around so that Shirley was facing the mirror.

Shirley studied the image carefully. The change was subtle, but pleasing. "I like it," she said. "It looks nothing like my mother's."

Debbie grinned. "Look closer, Shirley. Do you like the *entire* woman? The whole enchilada?"

Shirley looked back at the woman in the mirror. Enchilada wasn't that much of a stretch, but she had to admit, "I guess she's not all bad."

After Debbie, the milkman was going to be a cinch. He always came between seven and seven-thirty A.M.—right when Shirley was yelling at the kids to "Hurry and get ready or you'll be late for school!" They were usually yelling back about not being able to find something they needed. It was a family in early-morning turmoil, certainly not at its best. Life at that time of the day was chaos; and Shirley did not like exposing her family's chaotic dysfunction to outsiders like the milkman.

It wasn't as if he had just caught them on a bad morning. *Every* time this man approached the house to drop milk off on the porch, he was privy to the rantings and ravings of Shirley and her family.

This morning, the object of contention was a big pack of purple bubble gum and whether or not Sara could have it for breakfast. Shirley picked up a fit-pitching Sara and did her best to explain, "Grape gum does not count as one of your daily fruit requirements!"

"Put me down!" Sara screamed, scissoring her legs and swinging her arms until her mother's grip was undone. "Ouch! Why did you drop me?" Then the child went racing up the stairs, bellowing, "Daddy, Mommy dropped me! I think my legs are both broken!"

On such mornings, Shirley was almost always still in her pj's with no makeup and really scary morning hair. There had been that one morning some weeks back when she had gotten up early to impress everyone, but that just happened to be the milkman's day off.

He had been delivering milk to their home for a very long time now, and she just knew the man thought she never fed her family anything except cold cereal for breakfast, because half the time, they had to wait for him to deliver before they could eat. There were times when the kids even met him on the porch and told him so. If he had been a spy for the child welfare agency, Shirley suspected he would have turned her in as a negligent mother.

Then there was the matter of the milk bill. Not always, but sometimes, he had to bill her twice to get paid. The entire reason she had signed up for the program in the first place was because it was designed to save her trips to the grocery store. It was supposed to save her money, and it probably did, but it was one of those bills that did not come in the mail and often got lost or forgotten.

Shirley was sure the milkman thought she was a nagging wife and out-of-control mother. "Stan, why don't you help the kids with their homework for a change? Stan, why are you wearing that tie—you know it doesn't match. If I've told you once, I've told you a million times, HURRY! Look under the couch for your homework, kids. Can't you move any faster; you're going to be late for school again! I know we are out of eggs. That's just as well, because we're out of bacon, too. Just have another bowl of cereal. Sugar gives you energy."

Yes, Shirley was sure that the milkman rated her a generally rotten person.

She couldn't explain why, but she cared about what he thought, and was out to change his mind—to get him to validate her.

Why she felt the need to justify herself and her life to him, she could not explain. But she did. It wasn't like they had any relationship at all. He was the milkman. She was the customer.

Still, "milkman" was one of the pieces of her puzzle, and she was on a running campaign to complete the blasted thing now that she was so close.

This morning, she was the one who met him on the porch. She was wearing her skinny jeans—the ones she had to lie flat on her back to get zipped up. She had on a bright-red blouse. Debbie had told her red was a power color. It was supposed to give her self-confidence and be a warning to all who saw her that this was a woman to be reckoned with.

Her hair didn't look quite as good as it had when Debbie had styled it, but it still looked good. So—Stan had not noticed it. Big deal.

Her lips and eyes were lined and she was wearing gold hoop earrings and real perfume, not the rip-off imposter kind she usually wore, even substituting it once in a while for deodorant when she ran short on Extra Dry.

"Good morning," she greeted the milkman cheerfully. She wished that she could remember his first name, but wasn't even certain that she had ever known it in the first place. "I know I was a little slow in paying you last month, so here's this month's payment in advance."

He took the check and handed her two gallons of skim milk. "Thanks."

"Just in time for homemade French toast," she said. "My family loves my secret recipe. I put a teaspoon of vanilla in the batter."

He turned to leave.

"I know you must think I'm always a mess. You hear me screaming at my husband and children," she said, following him to his truck. "I know you must think all I feed my family is Froot Loops and Cap'n Crunch. I know you see me at my worst. You must think I'm a real slob, but I'm not. Honestly, I'm not."

Shirley was shouting now because the man was back in his truck with the motor running. His hand was on the gearshift.

He grinned down at her. "Actually, ma'am, I haven't given it a thought."

Shirley had to step away from the vehicle to keep from being hit as the milk truck shifted gears and continued down the street.

Stan met her halfway down the driveway. "What are you doing?" he asked.

Shirley burst out laughing, a hard and boisterous laugh.

"Now what?" Stan wanted to know.

Shirley kept laughing until tears were burning her eyes. She was laughing at herself. Why had she cared so much about the milkman's validation? Now that she had a broader perspective, she realized how absurd her concern had been. How much time and effort had been wasted. The man simply did not care enough to notice. He was too busy doing his job and going on about his life. What a healthy approach.

"What's so funny?" Stan asked, taking the milk from his wife.

"Just something the milkman said."

"A joke?"

"I suppose," she confessed. "The joke's on me."

"That's not all that's on you."

"What are you talking about?"

"Your hair."

Shirley smiled and patted him on the behind. "I was wondering if you were going to notice. Debbie cut it. It's a little *sassy*, wouldn't you say?"

He handed her back one of the gallons of milk. "Yeah, right. I especially like this effect," he said, tugging a huge wad of purple bubble gum from her hair.

Okay, so she had been totally wrong about the milkman, too.

The whole experience made Shirley promise herself that she would never address another person by saying, "I know you must think . . . "

So far, that sure knowledge of what other people thought had batted her zero. She did *not* know what other people thought, and to assume, she was beginning to realize, was not her prerogative.

The revelation here was that the people she

thought were thinking ill of her, were not really thinking *anything* of her. Zilch. Nada. Nothing at all.

Why she cared so much about what others thought of her was one of her major hang-ups. Shirley was beginning to realize that she had to care most about what she thought of herself. But would she ever truly understand that other people's opinions of her were a distant second to what she thought about herself?

Once she realized that impressing the milkman was not crucial to her validation, Shirley considered re-doing her puzzle. Maybe she should put her own name on one of the pieces. Maybe not. How could she validate herself?

She was thinking about that on the afternoon that her house cleaner was due. Shirley shut off the computer and got busy running her regular routine. She scrubbed toilets, vacuumed floors, dusted the mantel, and polished the glass in the china cabinet. She cleaned in preparation for the house cleaner. She always did. She still could not stand the thought of anyone thinking she was a slob.

She was too submerged in her familiar routine to realize the repetition of her efforts. Debbie. The milkman. Now the house cleaner.

"I'm sorry this place is such a mess," Shirley apologized, hiding a dust rag behind her back, "I've been so busy I've just had to let it go."

The young woman looked around at the freshly vacuumed carpet and the bleached kitchen counter-tops. "Don't worry about it."

Shirley struggled to keep the promise she had made to herself. Instead of declaring, "I know you must think I'm lazy, filthy, and a terrible home-maker," she did some fast rephrasing. "Do you think I'm lazy? Filthy? A terrible housekeeper?"

The house cleaner looked at Shirley like she was rabid.

Shirley hurriedly continued. "It's just that I feel so guilty for needing help. I feel inferior to all the women I know who work, raise families, and still maintain spotless homes."

"I haven't met any of those women in my line of work." She smiled at Shirley.

"Of course you haven't. I suppose you must think I'm a loon." Shirley sat down on the sofa and patted the cushion next to her, but the woman declined the invitation and remained standing.

"Shirley, I don't think you're a loon."

"I'm sorry. I have a bad habit of telling people what they think."

"I don't even know what a loon is."

"It's a reference to a crazy bird, but that doesn't matter. What matters is that I clear a few things up with you."

The woman stepped back and set down her bucket of cleaning supplies. "Have I done some-thing wrong?"

"No. No. Not at all. My approach on these things

is not clear. This isn't about you. It's about me. I'm trying to seek validation in my life and there are a few subjects that I'm very sensitive about. Housekeeping is one of them." Then under her breath she muttered, "My weight is another."

"I'm not following you."

"Let me explain. I care about what you think of me. Maybe I shouldn't, but I do. I think that's because you are the only person outside of my family who sees the skeletons I hide in the closets."

"Skeletons?"

Shirley waved her hands and the dust rag went flying. "Not real skeletons," she tried to explain. "It's just a figure of speech. I can close the door and hide my clutter to people who enter in only as far as the living room, but you see the clutter. You know I'm not the great housekeeper I pretend to be."

The woman nodded. "I think I understand now." Then she reached over and picked up the dust rag. "Shirley, you're hardly lazy or a bad housekeeper. The truth is, this is the easiest job I've got. You do all of my work before I ever get here."

"No, I don't!"

"Oh, yes you do. I sometimes wonder why you even have me come. I just know every woman needs a boost now and then."

This woman was so familiar with Shirley's personal domain—her kitchen, her bedroom, her bathrooms—that there were times Shirley had to admit, she felt a little intruded upon. That was not anyone's fault but her own.

"You seem to understand," Shirley said slowly. "You don't think I'm lazy? You don't think I just hire help so I can relax and let you do the work, do you?"

"Not at all. I have other clients whose houses are true disaster areas. We're talking dirty dishes, garbage, laundry, and junk. Those women don't apologize for having me come and help them. That's the point of my job, isn't it?"

"I suppose so," answered Shirley. "It's just that our budget is so tight, I feel guilty for spending any money on help when I should be doing the work myself."

"Are you firing me—is that what this is really all about?"

Shirley stood next to the woman. "No! What I am doing is trying to justify to you why I deserve your help. It really does give me that boost you mentioned."

"Shirley, you don't owe me any explanations. You work hard and I think you deserve all the help you can get. Besides, you don't pay me all that much."

Shirley had to look twice to be certain the woman was joking. She was. But then her tone turned serious. "I know my mother and both of my grandmothers hired help with their housework and none of them ever worked outside the home. My dad's mom talks about a day and age when women stayed in bed for three weeks after they had a baby. They hired help with their housework and cooking and they never felt guilty for it. She says every woman has a right to all the help she can get."

"Your grandmother sounds like a wise woman."

"I think so."

That made Shirley think about something she hadn't thought about all of her adult life. Her own mother had hired a teenage neighbor girl when Shirley was a child. The girl helped with the laundry and most of the heavy work. Money had been tight back then when Lena was adjusting to life as a new divorcee and a single mother, so having that extra help must have been a priority for Lena.

If Shirley's churning memory was working, she remembered that her maternal grandmother had had an actual live-in housekeeper to help with all of the chores, including raising Lena and her siblings.

"You know what?" Shirley said, her whole demeanor brightening. "I think I'm going to go pick up my little girl from preschool and take her to the park. I think I'll just leave you here to do your job."

"You mean you're not going to follow me around the house and help me clean like you usually do?"

"Not today."

"Sounds good to me. Have a fun time."

"I will," said Shirley. But before she left, she made a telephone call. "Hi, Mom. I just might not be the mighty tradition breaker that I think I am."

As she and Sara were walking hand-in-hand to the park, they ran into Mrs. Gleed, Shirley's favorite neighbor, and one of Shirley's all-time favorite people ever. The woman was a wonder. She was well into her eighties, but had the stamina of a teenager and the heart of a child.

"Hello, Shirley and Sara. You look like you're the best of friends."

"We are," said Sara. "Do you want to come to the park with us, Mrs. Gleed?"

"I've already been, honey. Just took my daily constitutional. Two miles and still going strong."

Shirley glanced down and noted the new jogging shoes. "You look like a kid, Nell," said Shirley. "That outfit matches your jogging shoes."

"My great-granddaughter gave it to me for my birthday. See the racing stripes?" She pointed to the red lines down the sides of her black pants. "They make me look faster than I actually am." She winked.

"I don't know about that." Shirley grinned. "You're too fast for me to keep up with."

"You really should come with me sometimes, Shirley. Exercise is good for the body as well as the soul."

"I'll do that, Nell."

"Then I'll stop by and pick you up next Monday. Don't be giving me any excuses when I get there, either."

"It's hard to say no to you."

"That reminds me. I wanted to thank you for the delicious chicken dinner you sent over with Sean on Sunday. I was feeling a little under the weather and hadn't made anything to eat. It really hit the spot. You just seem to know when people need you, and you meet their needs. You're quite a woman, Shirley."

Shirley shook her head. "It was nothing. Really it wasn't. I know the chicken was a little overdone and I'm sorry I didn't have anything else to offer you for dessert except that ice-cream bar."

Nell crooked her finger and waved it back and forth in Shirley's face. "Don't do that, dear. Don't discount all that is good about you. You are a wonderful woman. Now, I've got to run, but I'll see you on Monday."

Nell turned and Shirley watched as the woman power-walked down the sidewalk.

"Come on, Mommy," Sara tugged on Shirley's hand. "Let's walk fast like Mrs. Gleed."

While Shirley was swinging Sara, she thought about Nell Gleed and wondered why it was that whenever someone offered Shirley complimentary, validating words, they were quickly discarded, but if anyone said anything critical to Shirley, she guarded those words and harbored them safely in her memory.

Shirley decided to somehow work Mrs. Gleed into her puzzle. After all, the woman was a validator. She validated people in the way that she greeted them and treated them. Once Shirley felt validated she decided that she would follow Mrs. Gleed's lead and try to keep up with her footsteps. She, too, would become a validator and not just be content as a validatee.

Late that night, even after the dryer had stopped, Shirley lay awake—feeling better about herself than she could ever remember.

The afternoon in the park had turned into an evening picnic with the entire family. She came home to a clean house and no stress. Tonight she had soaked in a hot bubble bath and had shaved her legs with baby lotion. Stan had kept the kids occupied so she could have some time to herself. Pampered. Spoiled. She could get used to this.

At this very moment, Shirley felt she was the most blessed woman on the planet. She nudged Stan with her elbow. "Honey, are you awake?"

"Huh?"

She kissed him softly on the lips.

"I am now," he muttered.

"Will you do me a favor?"

"Probably. What is it?"

"I want you to validate me."

"What?"

"I want you to validate me." She had never dared to actually show him the puzzle and explain her undertaking, but his was the last piece of the puzzle. Once she had her husband's validation, the process would be complete.

"You want me to what?"

"I want you to validate me. Acknowledge me.

Love me. Appreciate me. Make me feel like a whole woman."

Now Stan sat up, rubbing the sleep from his eyes. "Shirley, you're up in the night."

She wrapped her arms around him and kissed his shoulder. "I know what time it is, but you're the last piece of my puzzle."

Stan didn't pretend to understand. He just reached over and took his wife in his arms. It was her favorite place to be. Then he cupped her face in his hands and kissed her, soft at first but then powerfully.

"How's that for validation?"

"It's a start," she said, falling backward, pulling him with her.

Three weeks later, Shirley was two weeks late. That scared her a little because her body worked to a twenty-eight-day cycle like a banker works nine to five.

"I think I might be pregnant," she announced to Stan, after she was sure he was sound asleep.

Wrong again.

Stan bolted up in bed like a wave of electricity had just run through him. "You think you might be *what*? When? How?"

"Pregnant. A few weeks ago. I think you know how."

There was an uncertain moment of dark silence before Shirley felt Stan's arms pull her close to him. "I know. It must have been that night you asked me to validate you."

"Probably," Shirley replied, "but that's not exactly what I meant."

"Sure it was," said Stan.

Shirley didn't respond. Men could be so . . .

. . . but then, so could women.

Stan held Shirley for a long, long time, assuring her how thrilled he was. Then he fell asleep, perfectly content. Shirley rolled him over onto his side and scratched his back until he started to snore.

She turned on the lamp by her bedside. Then she reached into her nightstand and took out a well-worn manila envelope. She scattered the contents on the quilt across her lap. She reached for the puzzle piece with Stan's name on it, but could not bring herself to glue it on to the matte board—not permanently, anyway.

Maybe that's because validation in a marriage was a two-way, never-ending process, she thought, as she worked with scissors, markers, and glue.

There was a new envelope lying there among Shirley's validation treasures. It had arrived earlier in the afternoon from the 1-900-VAL-DATE company. She opened it and read a once-in-a-lifetime offer to purchase a study course and video called "How to Seek and Find Validation." If she had any further questions, she could call the 1-900 number for only $3.95 per minute. What a deal!

Shirley crumpled the advertisement and tossed it into a nearby garbage can. Then she looked at her puzzle. It had not turned out at all like she had planned. There were pieces missing. Some changed. Others fit perfectly. More like a work-in-progress than the work-of-art that she had initially envisioned.

Shirley decided that tomorrow she would have it framed and then hang it proudly. The bathroom was still the most likely place.

Every time she looked at it, would she see how significant each piece was? What about the new pieces that would become necessary as new people entered her life? What about people who validated her without effort—people like Nell Gleed? What about the people who needed validation from her— that was an entirely different puzzle.

How mistaken she had been to imagine every piece would fit perfectly! That wasn't her life. That wasn't reality.

Reality was ever-changing, ever-learning, and ever-growing. Her life was a puzzle, and how boring it would be if all of the pieces were cut the same and fit neatly together.

As for validation, well, she wasn't quite sure she even understood the meaning of the word anymore. She suspected it was like love—a verb—a feeling that defied definition.

No, Shirley's validation puzzle had not turned out like she had planned. So what? She was learning to be grateful for life's little surprises.

Shirley tucked everything carefully back into her envelope, placed it in her drawer, turned out the light and snuggled up against Stan. She lis tened as the clothes dryer turned and turned and turned.

She snuggled closer to her husband and felt the warmth and strength of his body next to hers. Maybe tomorrow she would glue his puzzle piece down permanently.

On second thought . . . maybe she would just use Velcro.

In My Quest for Personal Growth, the Rest of Me Grew, Too

Shirley stepped onto the scale in her OB-GYN's office, carefully rocking from the balls of her tired, swollen feet to her cracked and calloused heels. Somehow she thought shifting her weight would lower the terrifying number that kept registering.

"What are we weighing in at today?" the nurse asked. *The 110-pound, never-been-pregnant nurse.*

Shirley was concentrating on keeping her balance, not to mention her bladder, under control. "*We,*" she replied with more sarcasm than intended, "think *your* scale is off."

The nurse grinned good-naturedly and then looked around at the six other pregnant women who were all staring blankly at Shirley.

Shirley wasn't about to be intimidated by them, and she couldn't help thinking, We'd make a great poster for *Save the Whales*. She almost said it aloud, but instead stepped off the scale and mumbled a number.

"What did you say?" the nurse asked.

"I said this week's grand total is . . . " Shirley cleared her throat and whispered that terrifying number.

The nurse furrowed her brow and looked disbelievingly at Shirley. "Um. Are you sure? Maybe our scale *is* off."

When the agony and humiliation of the doctor's appointment was finally over, Shirley took solace in the fact that only three weeks remained until her due date.

She refused to allow for the probability that she could go "over" her due date. Never mind the fact that her three previous children had all come at least one week late. That would not happen this time.

This pregnancy was so different from her first one. Shirley was now the mother of a teenager. Wasn't there some biological rule against that? Maybe her body had betrayed her, but if so, she was grateful for the double-cross. This baby was a blessing. If only it would just arrive before she faced every wife's nightmare of weighing more than her husband.

Three weeks.

Twenty-one days.

If this baby did not make its arrival by then, there were ways . . .

Hadn't her grandmother once mentioned something about a swig of castor oil and a very bumpy buggy ride?

"Excuse me, Shirley," the receptionist at the front desk asked as Shirley was waddling her way toward the exit. "When did the doctor say he wanted to see you again?"

"Next week," she answered.

The woman looked at Shirley sympathetically, or was it pathetically? Hard to tell.

"How about next Monday at ten A.M.?" the receptionist suggested. "It's the day after Mother's Day."

Shirley sighed as if to say, *Don't remind me.* Instead she responded, "How appropriate."

Later that afternoon, Shirley was again faced with the hearts, flowers, and chocolates of Mother's Day. She stood in the middle of the mall surrounded by a zillion reminders that it was once again time to pay homage to women with wombs.

Mothers.

Strange creatures.

Even though her current bloated condition and three living testaments at home qualified her as the recipient of such tribute, Shirley felt oddly detached from the masses honored one day each year.

It was the day Shirley dreaded.

Loathed was more like it.

Maybe this year she would let Stan babysit while she went to the marathon movie theater. Nope. Couldn't sit that long. Maybe she'd go to the local pub and play pool. That was out, too. In her shape, Shirley couldn't manage her belly up to the table to shoot.

Oh well . . .

Perhaps she could just feign the flu and slumber through those twenty-four hours. But she knew she could not do that, either. No. Shirley would have to remain awake to fully experience the fever, nausea and pain of that blessed day.

For a moment, Shirley almost forgot why she was surrounded by the insanity of the season and the madness of the mall. She had come to honor her own list of women—the mothers in her life.

But first things first. There was a baby sleeping on her bladder.

"Could you please tell me where the nearest rest room is?" Shirley asked someone who was sure to know—a woman pushing a stroller with one hand and dragging a toddler with the other.

The woman nodded to the left. "In the back of the bookstore right over there."

"Thanks. That's where I'm headed anyway."

Once nature's call was answered, Shirley knew she had another good thirteen minutes before it sounded again.

She headed straight toward the travel book section. She was shopping for her own mother, with whom Shirley was finally beginning to share validation after thirty-some years of being mother and daughter.

It was usually a bore to shop for her mom, but this year Shirley was glad for the can't-miss custom that had been established way back when Shirley was a teenager. Her mother would select her own present and all Shirley had to do was go pay for it.

This year it was a book about Hawaii. Why Hawaii, Shirley had no clue. Her mother was afraid of ships and planes. While standing in the cashier's line, Shirley began thumbing through the pages. It was filled with colorful photos of teenie-weenie bronzed women clad in string bikinis sprawled on white sandy beaches. "One of my thighs weighs more than two of those beach bimbos," Shirley muttered aloud.

"Did you say something?" the man ahead of her in line asked.

"Yes, would you please hold this and save my place?" Shirley shoved the book at him and headed back toward the rest room.

Next on the list came Stan's mother. The mother of all mothers-in-law. She and Shirley were not exactly friends, but they were not foes, either. In fact, Shirley's feelings for the woman fluctuated regularly. She was, after all, Stan's mother and the grandmother of their children. Oh well, that was a different subject altogether, and for the moment, Shirley had to keep focused on the task at hand.

"May I help you with something?" the department store clerk inquired.

"I'm looking for a gift for my mother-in-law."

"How about chocolates? We sell some of the finest in the world."

Shirley shook her head. "No. I always choose ones with the wrong nugget centers."

"How about clothes? Every woman loves a new outfit and we're having a great sale in the ladies' department upstairs."

"Clothes won't work," Shirley said. "My mother-in-law is roughly the size of our living room, but she is always insulted by the size we guess, and the color is *always* wrong."

"Have you considered perfume? One size fits all."

"Uh-uh. It doesn't matter what Elizabeth Taylor says, my mother-in-law thinks the perfume I choose stinks!"

The clerk finally chuckled and smiled knowingly. "I understand. I did my mother-in-law shopping yesterday."

"What did you buy?" Shirley asked eagerly.

"A gift certificate."

She paused for a moment, trying to think of ways her mother in-law could find fault with a gift certificate. "Great idea," she concluded. "I'll take one."

Enough energy expended on her mother-in-law. Why hadn't she gone generic and bought gift certificates for every birthday, Christmas, and Mother's

Day during the past decade and a half?

Shirley now shifted her attention as well as her belly. The baby had nestled off to one side. Shirley did her best to be inconspicuous in the middle of the mall as she laced her fingers together and hoisted the bottom of her belly from right to left. "Better," she groaned and continued on down the mall.

She had two grandmothers to shop for. Stan's grandma was a delight. No matter what she received, she did so with joy and appreciation. The kids could glue marshmallows to a piece of paper and she would act just as thrilled as the year the family bought her a new television set.

Shirley finally opted for a phone with extra-large glow-in-the dark lighted numbers and a red lighted button for numbers that were pre-programmed. They had tried a telephone once before with emergency and frequently-called numbers pre-programmed, but Grandma's eyesight was failing, so the three or four times a week when she tried to call Stan's family, she got the fire department instead.

Shirley suspected Grandma liked all of the attention, because there were always freshly baked brownies when the firemen arrived.

Shirley's own grandmother was not so easy to shop for. She lived in a retirement center, or "old folks' home" as she called it, confined by a broken arthritic hip to a wheelchair the woman detested.

Shirley's grandmother had been a USO entertainer during World War II. She had traveled the world bringing joy and laughter to people who really needed it. Now from her wheelchair, she continued to pound the piano every now and then and to belt out a tune or two to help cheer her fellow "inmates." But those tunes were coming less and less frequently.

Books were out. She couldn't see well enough to read and didn't like "stories on tapes." "It makes me feel like a little child who doesn't yet know how to read, so someone has to do it for me," she bemoaned. Shirley didn't see what was wrong with feeling like a child and being pampered, but Shirley's grandmother lived to do for others, and didn't like it when she was on the receiving end.

Shirley finally decided on a CD of Frank Sinatra's greatest hits. If Gran won't like it, her friends probably will.

Shirley also ordered flowers to be delivered on Saturday so they'd be fresh for Mother's Day. She got a little carried away and sent them to both grandmothers and six other women Shirley and her family had been mothered by. Among them were a neighbor, two women from church, and each of her children's homeroom teachers.

Shirley then headed back to the bookstore rest room and decided to do a little shopping for herself. She splurged. She bought a book on successful parenting, more because she was curious to know what *defined* successful parenting, than for any skills she hoped to acquire at this point in the game. She stopped by her favorite candy store and bought a couple of boxes of candy, just in case they forgot someone. She found a maternity store and bought a new bra—one that promised extra paneled support and a nifty opening for nursing mothers.

That was one good thing about being pregnant—she finally managed a chest of sorts. But the only time I get a chest is when my belly protrudes beyond my boobs. *Real* attractive, she thought.

She bought a new nightgown, equipped with windows for nursing mothers. It had only been four years since her last baby, but somehow Shirley's mind had blanked out all of the little reminders of pregnancy. Swollen leaking breasts, swollen sore ankles, and a swollen face that men liked to refer to as "radiant." And a forever swollen bladder.

The thought was enough to send her back to the bookstore.

Shirley could not help it. Once she started shopping, she had to remember *everyone* in the family. She knew the price she would pay when she got home if anyone was forgotten. Stan got a box of turtles, the kind made of milk chocolate, caramel, and pecans. They were Shirley's favorites.

Thirteen-year-old Samantha got a new pair of jeans. It didn't matter how many she had or that they all looked exactly alike, she never had enough. Seven-year-old Sean got a ball made of some weird sticky type of rubber so that when he threw it against his bedroom wall, it stuck. Shirley wasn't too happy with herself for that choice. By tomorrow afternoon it would be in the garbage. What a waste. But she kept buying little toys and then picking them off the floor the next day and tossing them. Mothers really were crazy. Four-year-old Sara was a lot like Gran. She was happy just as long as she was remembered. The price tag still didn't matter to her. What she really wanted was a turtle. A living, breathing, stinking, slimy reptile. Instead, Shirley bought a bow for her hair. It was green. She'd tell her it resembled a turtle and she'd share one of Stan's candy turtles with her.

With every purchase, the trip down the mall and out to the car looked more and more like it was not going to happen. Shirley had to keep stopping to rearrange her packages as the baby decided to practice gymnastics.

Shirley bit her lip, aghast at the thought that her water might break and she would go into labor in the middle of the mall. If she had been in the grocery store, she knew just what to do. Break a jar of pickles and waddle out unnoticed. But here? How was she going to explain . . .

She knew she had to get out NOW.

If she wasn't so panicked, she never would have done it. She would have taken the long, safe way out to the parking lot. Instead, Shirley opted for the short cut.

She forgot about the revolving doors until it was too late.

"Help!" she cried out when she realized she was stuck. Really stuck. Crammed in one of those little triangular glassed-in push-your-way-out cubies. Shirley, her belly, and eleven packages of varying sizes were all crammed in as neatly as dill pickles in a jar.

"Help!" she cried again. At this point, embarrassment gave way to claustrophobia.

The faces of strangers, young and old, gawked at Shirley as if they'd discovered an alien trapped, but no hand reached to help her. Not until Shirley heard the voice of a woman. A woman clearly in charge.

"Get out of the way!" the voice commanded.

The crowd parted and a woman dressed in a flowing forest-green cloak knelt down, unlodged the paper shopping bag that was wedged beneath the door, and released a nearly hyperventilating, but grateful, Shirley.

"Are you all right?" the woman asked once they were free from the crowd and as safe as one can be on the sidewalk outside a mall.

"I'll be okay now. Thank you for rescuing me. I feel like such an idiot. I am totally humiliated. I don't know what I was thinking. I'm as big as a heifer. I should have never attempted to—"

"Will you *stop*?" the woman laughed. "Actually, it was the highlight of my day."

Shirley looked at her rescuer for the first time.

Pencil-thin. Early forties. The auburn highlights were not from any sun in this universe. And the makeup, a little overdone, but applied meticulously. The clothes were nice. Real silk—from the fat worms in China, not from the skinny silk worms at WalMart. One glance saw that her nails were manicured professionally, her black pumps were new. The jewelry was genuine fourteen-karat, and there was no wedding band on the left hand.

Shirley must have stared a little too long.

"I didn't mean to make you uncomfortable," said the woman.

"It's a little late for that." Shirley laughed, too. "But my discomfort has nothing to do with you. Thank you so much for coming to my aid. I think the rest of the shoppers would have turned me into an amusement attraction."

"Can I help you to your car?"

Shirley handed her the largest and most awkward bags. "Thanks."

"My name is Rita. I just moved to town. The big divorce, you know."

"I'm Shirley. The big motherlode."

Both women laughed.

Before they parted, Shirley had given Rita her telephone number and invited her to lunch. She really hoped Rita would call. She and Shirley could not have been more different, but Shirley was in need of a good friend, not to mention a good lunch.

Check the Lost and Found, My Mind Is Missing

The remains of the day.

Yuck.

Just hours before, it had resembled dinner. Edible. Delectable. A real Thanksgiving feast. Now Shirley sat across the table from a mountain of dried-out cranberry sauce and congealed gravy. Plates stuck together between layers of mashed sweet potatoes, and mangled black olives that had served valiantly as finger puppets for the children. The bird of honor now looked like an abandoned carcass on the African plain. Picked over by the scavengers.

The mess was enough to depress anybody. Shirley propped her elbows on the table and wondered why she always insisted on this annual ritual. Every year since she and Stan had been married, in the teens now, Shirley had bid welcome to *all*. Her family. His family. The lonely people from their church. One year, Stan had even brought a homeless family in to dine with them.

Thanksgiving was never dull, that was for sure. The year Stan's grandfather and Shirley's great-Aunt Patti had recognized each other from a long-ago romance had really set the excitement precedent. Shirley tried to recall—wasn't it her great-uncle who had thrown the first punch? After that fiasco, this year would surely be considered a dud.

Now that everyone had gone home, and Stan and the kids were in front of the TV watching a video, a peaceful contentment filled Shirley's heart. She stuck her finger into a pie and licked whipped cream and spiced pumpkin.

"This is my idea of heaven," she said aloud. "I must be crazy."

"What are you saying?" Stan shouted from the adjacent family room.

"I was just talking to the turkey," she answered.

"Oh, I thought you were complaining about nobody helping you clean up the mess."

"What if I was?"

Stan took his time in replying. "I would be right by your side. I just don't understand why you never let our mothers help you clean up."

"I realize you don't understand, Stanley. Did you know that in some families the women prepare the Thanksgiving meal and then the men do all of the cleanup while the women watch football?"

Stan was suddenly behind her, rubbing her shoulders. "*What* families?" he asked.

"I heard about them on a talk show," she admitted.

"Figures. How would you feel if next year Sean

and Stephen and I were in charge of cooking Thanksgiving dinner?"

Shirley reached up and took his hand. "I don't think TV dinners would please your mother."

"What could she complain about? That the meat was dry, the potatoes needed more salt, and the rolls were too heavy?"

Shirley had to smile. "That's exactly what she said about today's meal. I didn't realize you were paying attention to the yearly critique."

"I hope you know she means well."

Shirley felt the muscles in her shoulders tense. She loved her mother-in-law, but it was not a subject she and Stan could ever talk about without Shirley feeling stressed and beaten.

"Do you want me to help you with the dishes?" Stan whispered.

"Sure," she replied, knowing very well that he was expecting her to pass on his offer. She stood and handed Stan a stack of dirty dishes, which he obediently carried to the kitchen sink.

"Anything else?" he asked.

"You can carve the rest of the turkey and take care of the carcass. You can put the rest of the food in Tupperware and put it in the refrigerator. You can scrape the plates and load the dishwasher. You can scrub the pots and pans and mop the floor. You can—"

"Okay, okay." Stan grabbed another load of plates and deposited them on the counter. Then he looked into the family room and announced, "I think little Stephen is waking up. I better go check him."

Shirley nodded. She knew her husband. Stan was never going to be domesticated. She attributed it to his upbringing and excused him because he once confessed that he was terrified of being the "yes-man" his father was.

Every once in awhile, the subject reared its ugly head, but for the most part, Shirley did what she felt needed to be done, and was grateful for the man that Stan was. Once in a while, she needed to be reminded, but times like this, when he ran from the kitchen like a terrified little boy, and headed for the couch where he cuddled his infant son, Stan's name topped her list of "things to be grateful for."

As soon as the dishwasher was loaded, the food in the fridge, and the floor swept, Shirley joined her family in front of the television. She collapsed on the sofa next to Stan and the baby. The rest of the kids were sprawled around the room. They were halfway through watching Jimmy Stewart discover what Shirley had felt all day.

She snuggled closer to Stan.

"You're in a good mood," he said.

"I'm feeling nostalgic," she admitted. "There's something about Thanksgiving night that makes me feel a little sentimental."

"There's something about Thanksgiving night that makes me feel a little hungry," he responded.

Shirley pulled away and sat upright. She looked at him. "You're joking, right?"

"No. A turkey sandwich with all the fixings sounds pretty good to me."

"Me, too!" Eight-year-old Sean suddenly emerged from the rug in front of the TV. "I want a turkey sandwich, with no cranberries."

"Is there any more fruit salad left?" asked Samantha, who was thirteen, and had been excused from helping with the cleanup, *only* because right after dinner she had claimed to have one of those mysterious teenage girl ailments. Something about aching all over and feeling "icky."

Shirley looked across the room at her first-born, who was in the middle of applying the umpteenth coat of magenta nail polish to her toenails. Samantha looked the picture of health to Shirley.

"I want some pumpkin pie with extra whipped cream," ordered Sara, who was pumping the rocking chair with her heels.

"Oh, you do, do you?" Shirley said. "For a four-year-old, you really know how to bark orders."

"And I want milk, too," Sara added.

Shirley sighed. "Didn't you people just stuff yourselves with enough food to last for the winter's hibernation period? Now that I have it all cleaned up and put away, you're ready to start again?"

As if on cue, baby Stephen started to squirm. Stan handed him to Shirley. "I think he's hungry," Stan surmised. "And he could use a changing."

Shirley cleared her throat as loudly as she could.

"Don't all jump up at once to help me. You might strain one of those muscles that you've been relaxing."

Stan reached over and took Stephen back. "Just kidding. I'll take care of the baby. Kids, you make your own leftovers, and fix a sandwich for me, please."

"Who is going to clean up?" Shirley asked with a smile.

They were all suddenly very engrossed in Clarence the angel's plight. Would he get his wings or not?

"It's a wonderful life, all right," she said.

Shirley's spirits were not dampened for long. The next morning, she was up before the rest of the family to greet one of her favorite days of the year—the beginning of the Christmas season. She never officially began the season until the day *after* Thanksgiving. Despite the commercialism of the holidays, Shirley had been brought up to believe there was something sacrilegious about tackling it too soon.

Every year she intended to shop the after-Christmas sales, in preparation for the following year. She just never got around to it. By the time Christmas was over, she was too drained—emotionally and financially.

This year, she vowed, would be different.

This year, she would actually *enjoy* the holidays.

This year, she would get her shopping done early. She would stick to her budget. Packages would be mailed the first week in December. The annual family Christmas card photo still needed to be taken. *That* she had put off on purpose, hoping that she could lose a few more pounds before it was time to mail them. Oh well, she might just send out a picture of the kids. Everyone had been asking for a photo of the new baby anyway.

The tree needed to go up right away. This year a living tree was her idea of saving the environment. The lights had to be hung and the decorations put up. Maybe this year Stan would actually hang the outside lights they had bought the first year of their marriage. Every year he said he would hang them, but never found the time. It was always too cold and the roof was always too high. For a few years, Shirley had threatened to hire someone else to hang their lights, but Stan talked her out of it, saying, "I have a plan for those lights. I want to put them all around the dormers and really make a statement." In the meantime, Shirley wondered if she could even find them, should Stan suddenly have the urge to ascend heights.

Shirley's mind was flooded with the anticipation and preparation for the holidays. There were parties, presents, and people that epitomized the season, and Shirley was looking forward to them all.

To get the season underway, she put one of Stan's battered tapes of the Mormon Tabernacle Choir's holiday favorites in the stereo. Then she poured some cinnamon oil in a saucepan and put it on the stove to simmer.

"It's beginning to look a lot like Christmas," she hummed.

Just then, the telephone rang. It was Stan's boss. He had to hold the line at least five minutes before Shirley was able to shake Stan from his slumber.

"It's my day off," he moaned. "Tell him I'm sleeping."

"He knows you're sleeping; that's why he told me to wake you. Still, I almost didn't. You looked like you were in the middle of some dream!"

"I was dreaming I actually had a day off without that jerk calling to suck my last thought." Stan rolled over and reached for the telephone on the nightstand next to the bed.

Shirley knew this scenario all too well. She knew that Stan was miserable working under his new boss. The man was a self-righteous cretin. But how was Stan supposed to walk away from a dozen years at the same company? Starting over in your twenties was exciting, but when you were double that age and starting over, it was the most terrifying thought in the world. A person only had so many times to start over. Her heart went out to her husband, and she could empathize.

Not today, though. Today she was going to launch the Christmas season with a bang.

When Stan came down the stairs, Shirley had the table set with red-and-green candles as Christmas centerpieces.

"They make the Cheerios look more festive." She attempted to solicit a smile from her husband.

No such luck. The look on his face made it clear that his day off had ended before it had begun. "I've got to go into the office this morning. Seems Curtis wants some help to finish 'his' proposal."

For one brief moment, Shirley was angry with Stan. This day was a *family* ritual! No work. Just play. How dare he defile this day-after-Thanksgiving tradition! But Shirley's anger dissipated as quickly as it came. She realized it was misdirected. She should be angry with Curtis, the insecure boss from hell. But Stan was angry enough for both of them.

Shirley looked into her husband's eyes and knew that he felt just as disappointed and deflated as she did.

"I hope I can be home by noon," he said without much conviction.

"The stores stay open late tonight so that might still work," she offered.

"Yes, but I know how you like to be first in line for the sales today."

"Maybe I'll just pack up all the kids and go to the mall anyway. I've been working on my shopping list, and this year, I've decided to get everything finished and out of the way so we can just relax and enjoy the season."

Stan put two pieces of bread into the toaster and didn't reply until they had popped up and he was spreading grape jelly on them.

He offered Shirley a bite of dripping toast.

She declined.

"Bah, humbug," he muttered.

As soon as Stan left for his office, Shirley blew out the festive candles and dialed her friend Rita's telephone number. She had met Rita a few months back, just before Stephen was born. The two had become fast friends, giving credence to the adage that opposites attract. In Shirley's mind, Rita was everything Shirley was *not*.

Rita was rich. She was eloquent. She was traveled. She was impeccable in her appearance. Shirley once went shopping with her and realized that Rita spent more on a single outfit than Shirley did on a month's worth of groceries. Granted, the ensemble included matching shoes and a purse, but still, the thought of spending so much on clothes made Shirley dizzy with guilt.

Yes, Rita was thin. Pencil-thin. Maybe that justified spending so much on a wardrobe. When you looked that good in a size five, why not?

If Shirley felt a little envious, it was because she was, although she would never admit it. What would it be like to trade lives for a day?, Shirley often wondered.

Rita was devoted to her career. She arranged financing for women's causes: everything from women's shelters to the rehabilitation program at the state correctional facility. Rita was obsessed with helping women in need. Her drive and endless motivation was still a mystery to Shirley. There was something behind Rita's obsession with helping women in need, but Shirley was still unraveling that mystery.

There were a lot of mysterious aspects about Rita that drove Shirley crazy. The woman was a closed book. Shirley was gradually beginning to read her and felt more and more grateful for their friendship. Just being around Rita made Shirley want to do more with her own life.

Rita was not driven by emotions like Shirley. Shirley ran on pure emotions. Rita, on the other hand, let her head rule her life. She did not lack direction. She managed to stay focused. She made a list of things to do, and had them checked off each night. Rita called it "prioritizing."

Right now, Shirley's priority was to get to the mall before all of the good stuff was ransacked.

When Rita didn't answer, Shirley went upstairs and woke Samantha.

"Rise and shine. It's Christmastime!"

Samantha rolled over and appeared to smother herself in her pillow.

"Get up, sleepyhead. I need your help."

"Aw, Mom. I don't feel well. I've got a stomach ache."

"That's too bad, because I'm going to the mall."

The pillow flew into the air and a sheet landed on Shirley's head. Samantha was out of bed, standing in front of the closet. "What am I going to wear?" she asked.

"I don't know, but I know I'm not wearing *this*," Shirley laughed, untangling herself from the forsaken sheet. "I washed your new jeans, the shredded ones with the holes in the knees. They're in the laundry room."

"Cool. Have you seen my red sweater?"

"It's there, too."

"Thanks, Mom. Can I call Heather and see if she wants to come with us?"

"If you think she's willing to help tend the kids while I do some Christmas shopping."

Samantha looked as though someone had just stolen her last piece of candy. "*Tend*? You mean I have to *baby-sit* at the mall?"

Shirley nodded.

"But Sean is such a brat. Sara whines all the time, and what if Stephen needs to be changed? I'm not changing diapers at the mall."

"We can take both strollers and trade off. If the baby needs to be changed, I'll do it."

"What about Dad? Why can't he at least tend Sean?"

"Because your father had to go to work today."

"I thought he had the day off. This was supposed to be a family day."

"I know. I know. But Curtis called, and your father had to go help him with a project."

"That guy's a geek. Dad should have just told him no."

"I think your Dad wishes he could."

"Why doesn't he?"

"Because Curtis is his boss. You don't tell your boss no."

"I would."

"I'm sure you would, my little unemployed teenager. Now get dressed, and I'll go wake up Sean and Sara."

After a quick breakfast of Cheerios with green milk (Sean's food-color contribution to the festive color scheme), the family piled in the minivan and headed to the mall. They arrived half an hour before the stores opened, but even then, parking places were about as scarce as a chocolate-sprinkled donut at a police officers' convention.

"This is ridiculous," Shirley complained, circling the parking lot for the third time. Finally, she decided to let the children out by the front door and then go park in a snow bank at the far end of the parking lot. "That way I won't have to drag the stroller and you kids across a half mile of filth and sludge. Now wait right by the front door," she instructed them.

When Shirley trudged across the parking lot, through the snow and crowds, she was horrified to find the children missing. No sign of Samantha or the strollers. No Sean. No Sara. No Stephen. She looked around at the ocean of people and wondered where to start searching. No one looked like mall security, but everyone suddenly looked like mass murderers.

She couldn't help it. Tears welled up in her eyes. There was no worse feeling in the world to a mother than to not know the whereabouts of her children.

Shirley started screaming. "Samantha! Sean! Sara! Stephen!" She jumped up and down in an attempt to look over the crowds. Maybe Samantha had just found one of her friends and wandered off. Maybe Sara had been stolen and the rest of the kids were chasing the kidnapper. Maybe Sean had seen a toy he wanted and taken off. Why, why had she been so foolish to leave them by themselves, even for a few brief minutes?

The tears were flowing freely now as people passed by unaware of her dilemma. She was about to stop and scream for the police when she heard a familiar voice.

"Mom! You said you would change him!" It was Samantha, indignant, but safe, and flanked by the other children. "As soon as we got in here, Stephen started to stink up the whole mall. So we went to the bathroom to change his diaper. You owe me one."

Sara stared up at Shirley from the stroller. "Sean drives too fast. We about ran an old lady over."

"I do *not* drive too fast!" Sean protested. "I missed that old woman by a mile. Hey, Mom, I saw a Mountain Monster Masher in the toy store down at the end of the mall where we can have our picture taken with Santa Claus. You know how bad I want a Mountain Monster Masher. It's the only thing I really want for Christmas."

"Are you crying, Mommy?" Sara asked.

Shirley wiped the tears from her cheeks and tried to swallow the lump in her throat. "Let's go Christmas shopping!" she managed, placing a hand on both strollers. "And don't leave my sight again!"